Elle Woods

Vote Blonde

Elle Woods

Vote Blonde

Based on the character
created by Amanda Brown

Story by Natalie Standiford

HYPERION PAPERBACKS FOR CHILDREN
New York

Copyright © 2006 by Amanda Brown

First Edition

1 3 5 7 9 10 8 6 4 2

Printed in the United States of America
Library of Congress Cataloging-in-Publication Data on file

ISBN 0-7868-3887-6

Visit www.hyperionbooksforchildren.com

Elle Woods

Vote Blonde

Chapter 1

"IT'S so good to be back!" Elle Woods said as she stepped through the school doors for the first time that fall. "Ah—Breathe in that delicious school hall-way air."

She stopped to take it all in—her first day back at Beverly Hills High School: the hustle and bustle, the new faces, the familiar ones, the brand-new clothes . . . And speaking of new clothes, she took pleasure in her new pair of perfectly worn jeans and new lacy blue tank top. It was good to feel dressed exactly right for the occasion.

"Takes you back, doesn't it?" Elle said to her best friend, Laurette Smythe.

"Back to what?" Laurette said. "Tenth grade? That

was only three months ago."

"Feels like a lifetime," Elle said. She took another deep breath. "BHH has its own particular perfume."

"Perfume?" Laurette said. "All I smell is sloppy joes and brussels sprouts. I'd rather be at the beach breathing in fresh, salty air."

"Who wouldn't?" Elle said. She loved the beach, and had spent the summer learning to surf, among other things. "But you have to admit there's something exciting about a new school year. We're juniors now. We know what's what. No surprises for us. We're ready to rule the school."

"I guess," Laurette said. She was wearing new clothes too, in a way. Her striped velvet pants and matching jacket had been made in the seventies, but she'd just bought them at a vintage shop the week before. "I miss Darren already. Don't you miss Hunter?"

Darren Kidd was Laurette's boyfriend, and Hunter Perry was Elle's. Both boys had graduated that spring and had just started college. Hunter was at nearby UCLA, and Darren was farther away, at University of California, Santa Barbara.

"Of course I miss Hunter," Elle said. "I wish he could be here—that would make the school year perfect. But since he isn't, I'm going to keep busy. There's so much to look forward to! Cheerleading, and football games, and Homecoming, and the Homecoming Dance . . ."

"So you're going to try out for the squad this year?" Laurette asked.

The year before, Elle had helped transform the cheerleading squad from dishwater dull to bright and shiny, even though she wasn't a cheerleader herself.

"Definitely," Elle said. "Want to come? Tryouts are this afternoon after school."

"No, thanks," Laurette said. "And I think you know why."

Elle nodded. "I understand." Laurette wasn't the cheerleading type. All that pep gave her indigestion. She didn't hold Elle's cheeriness against her, though.

A familiar bologna smell suddenly overpowered the sloppy joes and brussels sprouts. Elle braced herself, because she knew what, or who, couldn't be far behind: Sidney Ugman.

"Elle, you look more stunning than ever," he said. "You're aging so gracefully."

"Aging? She's sixteen, Sidney," Laurette said.

"I didn't mean that you're old," he said to Elle. "I only meant you get cuter every year. Wish I could say the same for every girl at BHH." He looked meaningfully at Laurette.

"I wish I could say it about any of the boys," Laurette said. "Most of them peaked in third grade."

Sidney lived next door to Elle in Brentwood and had had a crush on her since kindergarten. A major crush. Elle tried to be nice to him, but he tested her patience. He was awkward and tubby—and his bologna smell really bothered her. He'd been away at computer camp all summer, which had been like a bologna-free vacation for her nose.

"Who do you have for homeroom this year?" Sidney asked. "Myer?"

Elle checked her schedule. Rats, she thought. She did have Mr. Myer for homeroom. That meant another year of finding creative ways to avoid sitting next to Sidney every morning.

Laurette looked at her own schedule, then Elle's. "We both have Myer. El Comb-over. Room 243." Mr. Myer was known as "El Comb-over" because he was completely bald except for a long lock of hair that started on one side of his head and wound up plastered over the rest of his skull. Elle thought it was sad. If only he had cut that thing off and embraced his baldness, she thought, he might have been decent-looking.

The bell rang. It was time for the first homeroom of the semester.

"Guess we'd better go," Sidney said. "Where will you be sitting, Elle?"

Elle hugged her books to her chest to keep them from getting contaminated by Sidney. New books had a nice, fresh, papery smell that faded all too quickly. "I'm not sure yet," she said.

"She's sitting with me," Laurette said.

They headed for homeroom to start their new school year. Elle had high hopes for it.

Ready? Let's go!" Elle chanted a new cheer she'd written for the Beverly Hills Killer Bees cheerleading squad. Last year had been all about basketball, but now Elle was thinking football. New sport, new cheers.

"You don't really have to try out, Elle," Chloe Gaitskill said. "We all know you're good. You totally transformed the squad last year. If you want in, you're in."

The other cheerleaders nodded and murmured in agreement. But Elle said, "No, I want to do things the right way. The official way. So watch me try out, and if you think I'm good enough, take me on."

"Elle is right," Chessie Morton said. "We shouldn't

play favorites. We need the best cheerleaders on the squad, not just the girls we like."

This comment was greeted with silence. Chessie was the most enthusiastic yet clumsiest girl on the squad. But no one wanted to hurt her feelings—or get on her bad side—by pointing that out.

Chessie looked up to the top cheerleaders and desperately wanted to be like them. She had followed Savannah Shaw, last year's captain, around like a puppy. This year her idol was Chloe, who seemed to be the obvious choice for captain.

"Thanks for taking my side, Chessie," Elle said. "Wait till you hear this new cheer, though. You're all going to flip!"

She paused, composing herself.

> *Ready? Let's go! Go, Bees, let's go, Bees, sting those Speedsters in the knees, flood their engines, pop their tires, cut all their ignition wires, take the field, run down and score. Touchdown! Touchdown! Give us more! Go, Bees!*

Elle did funky dance moves while she chanted, ending in a backflip. She'd practiced hard all summer to get it right. Tumbling didn't exactly come naturally to her. She had to work at it. She was better at designing outfits and writing funny cheers.

"Yay!" All the cheerleaders applauded, except for Chessie.

"You've really improved, Elle," Chessie said. "Remember last year, when you couldn't even do a flip? Now you're almost up to our level!"

"I think she's great," Chloe said. "And she's the most motivated girl on the squad. I nominate Elle for captain."

Chessie's jaw dropped. She'd assumed that that honor would go to Chloe. But if it didn't, she wanted a chance at it.

"Chloe, you're so generous," Chessie said. "But you're the best girl for the job, don't you think?"

Chloe shrugged. "It's too much work. I like being a cheerleader, but I don't really feel like making up new cheers or organizing road trips. I say, if Elle wants to do it, let her."

"Maybe we should take other nominations," Chessie said. "Does anyone else have a candidate they want to suggest?"

Chessie stood in the middle of the group, posing, her hands on her hips. Elle could see that she really wanted to be the captain.

"I do," Elle said. "I nominate you, Chessie."

Chessie seemed a little confused by this. "Don't you want the job?"

"Sure I do," Elle said. "But I want what's best for the team. If the others think you'd be a better captain, then that's what's best."

"I'm sold," P.J. said. "I vote for Elle."

"Me, too," Tori said.

"All in favor of Elle, say aye," Chloe said.

"Aye!" everyone responded, except Chessie.

"Wait a minute! I didn't get a chance to show what I can do!" Chessie protested.

"We know what you can do, Chessie," Chloe said. "Vote's over. Elle, you're captain."

"Wow!" Elle hadn't expected this. Captain! "I'm honored. Thank you. I promise I'll do my very best."

Chloe picked up the *Cheerleader's Rule Book* and held it in one hand like a Bible. "Time for your official induction," she said to Elle. "The Cheerleader's Oath. Place your hand on the rule book and repeat after me."

Elle proudly put her hand on it. This was a big moment.

"I, Elle Woods—" Chloe prompted.

"I, Elle Woods . . ."

"Do solemnly swear . . ."

"Do solemly swear . . ."

"To be the best cheerleader I can be."

Elle followed Chloe, repeating everything she said. "To practice faithfully and diligently, to keep my uniform neat and clean, to look my best at all times, to catch the fliers and spot the torches, to give the squad a steady base so we can all fly high. Most of all, I promise to be loyal to my school, my team, and my fellow cheerleaders. A cheerleader is honest and true. Go, Bees!"

"Go, Bees!" the other cheerleaders said in unison, solemnly, with their hands on their hearts.

"Welcome to the squad," Chloe said.

"Thank you," Elle said. "I promise to uphold the principles of the Cheerleader's Oath in everything I do."

"You don't have to go overboard," Chloe said. "Just don't do us wrong."

"I won't," Elle said.

"Sit with us, and watch the rest of the auditions," Chloe said. "There are only two spots open on the squad. You're captain, so you should decide which of the new girls gets them."

Elle sat with the rest of the squad members and watched as girl after girl, mostly freshmen, tried out for those two precious spots. It was hard to decide; several of the girls were very good.

"Thank you, girls," Elle said when the tryouts were over. "We'll post our decision tomorrow morning. You were all great. It's going to be so hard to choose only two!"

She dismissed the girls, taking to the role of captain very quickly, and discussed them with her teammates. Finally, they agreed on two freshmen: Lisi Washburn and Tamila Vines.

"I'll go post the notice in the school building right now," Elle said. "So the girls will see it first thing tomorrow when they come in."

"Elle, have you decided who you want for your cocaptain?" Chessie asked.

"There's a cocaptain?" Elle said. "I didn't know."

"There's no cocaptain," Chloe said.

"But there could be a cocaptain," Chessie said. "Or a vice-captain. Whatever. If Elle wanted one."

"Okay, Chessie," Elle said. "You can be my vice-captain. See you guys tomorrow."

Elle left the gym and went to her locker in the main school building. She wrote out her team announcement in bright blue letters, decorated with gold. (Blue and gold were the school colors.) Then she went to the bulletin board to post the notice.

A boy stood at the bulletin board, stapling a large poster to it. He was pale and doughy-looking, as if he spent a lot of time indoors, which was an anomaly in sunny southern California. He had wire-rimmed glasses and brown hair cut short like a little boy's, even though he was a seventeen-year-old senior. He wore his pants buttoned high on his waist, with his shirt tucked in, but not in an ironic hipster way—just a plain old goofy way.

Elle knew who he was; everyone did. His name was Curt Blaylock. He was the student body president and was widely considered the smartest boy in school.

Elle pinned her announcement to the board, then stepped back to read Curt's. It said, REELECT BLAYLOCK FOR PRESIDENT.

"Do I have your vote?" Curt asked Elle.

"Who's running against you?" Elle asked.

"The other candidates haven't been announced yet," Curt said. "But I doubt that anyone else will make a serious bid. Nobody would dare. I'm a shoo-in."

Elle knew that Curt was probably right. In spite of her best efforts, a strong strain of apathy ran through Beverly Hills High School. Furthermore, the role of student body president wasn't exactly a coveted position. The school president was never cool. And nothing was more important to Beverly

High kids—most of them, anyway—than being cool.

"Well, if no one runs against you, then I'll vote for you, for sure," Elle said.

"Thanks."

"If you're elected, what will you do?" Elle asked.

"Same as last year," Curt said. "Nothing new. But I do have one big improvement I want to make to the school. I think I'll get a lot of support for it, too."

"What's that?"

"I'm going to abolish all school dances," Curt said. "All of them. And Homecoming will be the first to go."

"What?" Elle thought he must be kidding. How could he abolish school dances? It was crazy. Who would want that?

"What good are they?" Curt said. "Nobody likes them. They're a waste of money—money that could be spent on something way more fun, like a *Star Wars* trivia marathon."

"A *what?*" Elle was stunned. Was he serious?

"I say their time has come and gone. No more dances. And if elected, I'll make sure of it."

Elle was so shocked she hardly knew what to say. No dances? It was barbaric!

Chapter 2

"ELLE, GET a grip," Laurette said. "You'd think this was the end of the world as we know it."

"But it is!" Elle said. "No dances? What's the point of going to school?"

"To learn stuff?" Laurette ventured. She and Elle were discussing Curt's campaign promise at lunch the day after Elle had heard about Curt's plan.

"We take classes, sure," Elle said. "We learn things. But we can do that anywhere. There's more to school than that. There's a reason we come to this building every day."

"I know," Laurette said. "So the teachers can torture us and we can torture them back."

"No, silly. Social stuff," Elle said. "Hanging in

the halls. Lunchroom real estate. Community service. Sports teams. Cheerleading. And best of all, dances. Without dances, we might as well be homeschooled!"

"I wish I were homeschooled," said P. J. Stoller, who had just pulled a chair up to the table, along with Chessie. "No way would my mother ever make me suffer through Chemistry. Too messy."

"If I were homeschooled, I'd be really bad at math," Laurette said. "And really good at making fancy blender drinks."

"I'm serious, you guys," Elle said. "Aren't you upset? If Curt wins the election we won't have any more dances—ever! And he'll probably win. The only person running against him is Merlin Jones, and he doesn't have a chance."

"Not even the marching band would vote for Merlin," P.J. said. "He's too weird."

Merlin Jones—his real name, and he did his best to live up to it—kept his hair in a flat, monkish bowl cut and usually wore a wizard's cape to school. In addition, he wore his extra-wide black band shoes everywhere. He was an excellent tuba player.

"Why does he even bother?" P.J. said.

"I think he likes campaigning," Chessie said. To

Merlin, campaigning meant walking around school playing the tuba. He ran for every office in the school: Prom King, Homecoming King; student senator; and head of every committee, from the social ones to the ones dealing with community service. No one ever voted for him, but he tootled around with his tuba playing "Happy Days Are Here Again" and wearing a sandwich board that said, A VOTE FOR MERLIN IS A VOTE FOR MAGIC.

"A vote for Merlin is a vote thrown away," Laurette said.

"Everyone knows Curt's the smartest boy in school," Elle said. "But I don't understand why he'd want to abolish dances. Why does he care so much?"

"I bet I know," Laurette said. "Because he's never been to one. Ever. He's never been able to get a date."

"And neither have any of his friends," Chessie said.

"But he's not bad-looking," Elle said. "All he'd have to do is wear his pants a little lower, and I'm sure he could get a date, if he really wanted one."

"Maybe his standards are too high," Chessie said. "He asked me to the Valentine's Day dance two years ago. *Me*. What was he thinking?"

"What did you say?" Elle asked.

"I said, 'As *if*,'" Chessie said.

"Who did you end up going with?" asked P.J.

"Nobody," Chessie said. "But I wasn't about to go with *Curt*. He's okay, but I was shooting for—" She stopped and threw a glance at Elle, who knew the name Chessie was about to mention: Hunter. Chessie had always liked him. Lots of girls did. He was gorgeous, talented, and sweet.

"—Someone more popular," Chessie finished.

"Huh," Laurette said. "So you *are* capable of tact."

"No wonder Curt hates dances," Elle said. "Getting rejected all the time must hurt."

"Nobody really cares about the stupid dances anyway," P.J. said. "This is L.A. If I want to go dancing I can just go to Pacifico or one of a zillion other clubs. Nobody cool goes to dances anymore. They're totally lame."

"I can't believe I'm hearing this," Elle said. "I went to Prom last spring, and it was the greatest night of my life."

She would never forget it. Hunter, her dream boy, had taken *her* to the Senior Prom. It was their very first date. She had felt like a princess that night.

"Hey, wait a second," Chessie said. "If Curt

cancels all dances, does that mean no Homecoming Dance?"

"Yes," Laurette said. "Did you think he'd make an exception for Homecoming?"

"Well, kind of." Chessie's expression had changed from the usual smug boredom to dawning horror. "I was counting on a Homecoming Dance."

"Why?" Elle asked.

Chessie looked at her as if she'd asked a really stupid question, like why Chanel was better than Payless. "Because I'm going to be Homecoming Queen this year," she said.

"You are?" P.J. said.

"How do you know?" Laurette asked.

"Duh! I'm going to run for it," Chessie said. "Of course I'll win. I've got to. It's my dream."

"I thought your dream was to be captain of the squad," P.J. said.

"Not anymore," Chessie said, elbowing P.J. "As of yesterday, this is my real dream."

"That's great, Chessie," Elle said. "But if Curt wins, there won't be a dance."

"Now I understand what all the fuss is about," Chessie said. "It's all starting to make sense. A Homecoming Queen wouldn't have much to do without a dance to preside over."

"Exactly!" Elle said.

"It's a nightmare come true," Chessie said.

"We have to make people understand," Elle said. "No club can make up for the thrill of a school dance. Seeing the kids you pass in the halls every day all dressed up, showing a different side of themselves. Acting like royalty for a night. The tension and anticipation—Will the boy I like ask me to dance? Will he kiss me?"

"Will I make a complete fool of myself?" Laurette added. "That's always part of the entertainment."

"Remember last year when Aaron tried to break-dance and ripped his pants?" P.J. said.

"That was a good one," Chessie said. "He didn't realize it, and nobody told him till the end of the night that his Pokémon underpants were showing."

"That's what I mean," Elle said. "Everyone talks about a dance for days—weeks—afterward. It can change the chemistry of the school. Popular people might lose some of their luster. Unpopular people might suddenly shine. Going to a dance is the right of every American high school student. We can't let it slip away without a fight. And I for one am going to find a way to stop Curt from putting his evil plan into action."

"Very inspiring, Norma Rae," Chessie said. "But how are you going to do that? Curt is unbeatable. He *will* be reelected. And once he's president he can slide whatever new rules he wants right through. After all, nobody goes to student senate meetings."

"Except his nerdy friends," Laurette said. "And they do whatever he tells them."

"Bunch of yes men," P.J. said.

"I can't believe how apathetic we all are," Elle said. "We just accept the way things are because we think we can't change them. But we can. We have the power, if we try hard enough."

"How?" Chessie said. "What can you do?"

That was the question that had Elle stumped. What *could* she do? How could she stop Curt if nobody else cared?

"There is one solution," Laurette said. "But it's a long shot."

Good old Laurette, Elle thought. "What is it?" she asked.

"You could run," Laurette said, "for student body president."

Chessie laughed. "Elle? Student body president? I knew you were funny, Laurette, but that's the best joke I've heard in ages."

"She's right, Laurette," Elle said. "Who would ever vote for me? Over Curt?"

"You know I think you're sweet," Chessie said to Elle. "And you'll be an awesome captain of the cheerleading squad." She coughed a little and cleared her throat. "But if we're going to keep dances alive, we need to come up with a plan that will actually work."

"Do you have any ideas?" Laurette asked.

"No," Chessie said. "All I know is if Elle runs for school president she'll be making a fool of herself, and wasting her time. She can't win."

"Really," P.J. said. "A cute blonde cheerleader for president? It's never happened before."

"Maybe someone like Savannah Shaw could have pulled it off last year," Chessie said. "She had so much style." Savannah Shaw had been an über-popular former captain of the cheerleading team and Chessie's idol, until she graduated. If she wore a newsboy cap, or green sparkly eye shadow, the style would instantly become a new fashion craze and sweep the school.

"She practically had mind control," Laurette said.

"Elle, don't get me wrong," Chessie said. "I like you. But you don't have the kind of personal magnetism that wins elections. You only just stopped being a complete loser a few months ago. Until last spring you were practically invisible."

"Remember those baggy clothes you used to wear?" P.J. said.

"All someone has to do is find a photo of you with those big glasses and mousy hair, and you're finished," Chessie said.

"I don't agree," Laurette said. "Elle's transformation could be an inspiring backstory. You know, 'I started from nowhere and pulled myself up by my bootstraps to get to where I am today.'"

"Ick. Please," Chessie said.

"I know it's an uphill battle," Laurette said, "but I think Elle could beat Curt, with a properly managed campaign."

"Laurette, please be my campaign manager," Elle said. "You have so many great ideas! I'll be lost without you."

"I accept the challenge," Laurette said.

"So you're actually going to do this?" P.J. asked.

Elle thought about it. She knew she probably wouldn't win. But would that be so bad? Wasn't the important thing to try one's best?

"Yes," she said. "I'm going to do it. I'm running for president!"

"Hooray!" Laurette said.

"Oh, my gosh," Chessie said. She touched Elle's forehead to see if it was warm. "You don't have a fever. That makes it official: you've lost your mind."

"No, I haven't," Elle said. "I've found my inner candidate." She jumped up on the table. "I, Elle Woods, hereby declare myself a candidate for president of the Beverly Hills student body. If elected, I promise to make this school a nicer place, a prettier place, a happier place. New paint on the walls, in tasteful colors like lavender and mauve. No more beige and brown! Planters in the classroom windows, with real live flowers in them. A dress code for teachers, banning all pleated slacks, dowdy skirts, and crepe-soled shoes. Comb-overs will be banned for all male teachers and administrators. If you're bald, you're bald. Face it."

"That means you, Mr. Myer," Laurette said.

"And most important of all—" Elle paused dramatically, to make sure she had everyone's attention. "A date for every student to every dance—guaranteed!"

The rest of the kids in the lunchroom had stopped what they were doing to listen to Elle's stump speech. They laughed and applauded, thinking it was a joke. But Elle was dead serious.

"A date for every student to every dance?" Chessie said.

"As your campaign manager, I advise you against making that promise," Laurette said. "How will you ever keep it? It could blow up in your face."

"It doesn't matter," Chessie said. "If you don't win the election, you don't have to keep your campaign promises. And trust me, Elle, you won't win."

"We'll see about that," Laurette said.

"Yeah, we'll see," Elle said. She tried to sound tough, but inside, she knew Chessie was probably right. Elle for student body president? What was she thinking?

Chapter 3

"PRESIDENT PUSSYCAT," Elle's father, Dr. Wyatt Woods, said after Elle told her parents about her plan. "It has a nice ring to it."

"I can't believe you're running for school president," her mother, Eva, said. "I thought you wanted to be popular."

"She *is* popular, dear," Wyatt said. "Aren't you, pussycat?"

"Kind of, I guess," Elle said. She sat on the couch, stroking her toy Chihuahua, Underdog.

"Wouldn't your time be better spent on cheerleading, and maybe chairing the social committee? How about holding a charity event? A few years ago the Beverly girls had a lovely fashion show—"

"Mom, if Curt Blaylock wins the election there won't be any social committee. He wants to abolish all school dances."

"How awful!" Eva said.

"That seems like an odd platform to run on," Wyatt said. He sucked on his pipe. "Aren't there any more important issues than that at your school?"

"Not according to Curt," Elle said. "He hates dances."

"He must be power mad," Eva said. "Being president has gone to his head."

"Maybe so," Elle said. "That's why I want to stop him."

"Well, let us know if we can do anything to help," Eva said. "Want me to have some key mothers over for cocktails? I'll have the ears of the mothers of the most influential movers and shakers at school."

"I don't think most of the movers and shakers listen to their mothers," Elle said. "No offense."

Eva looked shocked. "What happened to 'Mother knows best'?"

"About school politics, I mean," Elle added quickly.

"I could hold a fund-raiser," Wyatt said. "You'll need big bucks to fight a sitting president. He's got all the school resources at his disposal—"

"Thanks, Dad," Elle said. "I'll let you know. In the meantime, I thought I'd make some posters and buttons."

"That's sweet," Eva said. "I'll help you." She rang a bell and Zosia, the maid, and Bernard, the butler, appeared. "Elle is making campaign posters, and she needs help."

"No, I—" Elle began, but her mother was already on a roll.

"So I'm helping her by asking you two to do whatever you can," Eva said.

"I'm good at posters," Bernard said. "I can draw a perfectly straight line, freehand."

"How much are they paying you to run?" Zosia asked. "You're the lame duck, right?"

"The what?" Elle said.

"When I was a little girl in Poland, before we got democracy, we had elections, but usually there was only one candidate," Zosia said. "When there were two, it was just for show. The loser—the lame duck—got paid or got a cushy government job. What will you get?"

"I'm hoping to win," Elle said.

"Against that boy Curt Blaylock?" Zosia laughed. "He's a born politician! He already has a seat on the Beverly Hills zoning commission."

Elle was amazed. "He does?"

Zosia nodded. "I know because one of my friends tried to hold a running yard sale in her driveway."

"A running yard sale?"

"Okay, it was kind of like a store in her yard. She had a lot of stuff," Zosia said. "That Blaylock boy shut her down like Kevin Costner in that movie about guys who go around shutting things down."

"*The Untouchables*?" Elle asked.

"Yes," Zosia said. "Curt went after her like a pit bull. Fines, lawsuits . . . You'd think she had a speakeasy in her garage."

"Just because she was selling her stuff in her driveway?" Elle asked.

"I can understand that," Eva said. "You don't want junk sales going on in people's yards. It cheapens the neighborhood. This is Beverly Hills, not a trailer park."

"This Curt sounds like a tough opponent, pussycat," Wyatt said. "Better make those posters good."

"Make sure you use lots of gold and silver paint," Eva said. "People love metallics. They attract attention." She owned an art gallery and knew about such things.

Elle's cell phone rang. She checked the ID—it was Hunter!

"I'll take this in my room," Elle said, rushing upstairs to her bedroom.

"Hey," Hunter said.

Elle melted at the sound of his voice.

"How's it going? How's Beverly this year?"

"Great," Elle said. She had a lot of news for him. "I was voted captain of the cheerleading squad."

"Congratulations!" Hunter said. "Not that I'm surprised. You are the best thing that ever happened to that squad."

"Thanks," Elle said. "I've got even bigger news. I'm running for school president."

"You're kidding!" Hunter said. "Did Blaylock get hit by a truck or something? I thought he wanted to be president for life."

"No, he's fine," Elle said. "I'm running against him."

"Wow." Elle could tell that Hunter was impressed. Either that or he couldn't believe her nerve. "That's going to be a tough race."

"I know," Elle said. "But I had to do it. He wants to abolish dances. All dances. Forever!"

"What about Homecoming?" Hunter said. "We're

still going to go together, right?"

"Not if Curt has his way," Elle said. "But enough about boring old high school. What's happening at college?"

"It's great," Hunter said. "But it's tons of work. So much more than high school. And I'm going out for the basketball team, and a frat is rushing me—Sigma Chi. I barely have time to sleep."

"But you love it, right?"

"I love it. But I miss you," Hunter said.

"I miss you, too," Elle said.

She heard the doorbell ring, and a minute later Zosia knocked on her door. "Elle? Laurette is here."

"Laurette's here to help me start my campaign," Elle told Hunter. "Guess I'd better go."

"Have fun," Hunter said. "And good luck. I believe in you, Elle."

After she hung up, she sat still for a moment luxuriating in the warm Hunter feeling. It was like soaking in a hot, fragrant bath. Then she went out to the living room. It was time for Team Elle to get to work.

"How's Hunter?" Laurette asked when Elle walked in.

"How did you know I was talking to him?" Elle said.

"The dreamy look on your face," Laurette said. "It's a dead giveaway."

Things quickly fell into place as the two girls proceeded to plan the campaign. Elle was good at designing things, so she was in charge of the posters. Laurette made sure they had plenty of supplies. She was also in charge of making copies of buttons and flyers with Elle's campaign slogan on them. She and Elle came up with a number of potential slogans:

> VOTE WOODS—SHE'S GOT THE GOODS.
> BLONDES HAVE MORE FUN—AND SO WILL YOU,
>   WHEN YOU ELECT ELLE WOODS FOR
>   PRESIDENT.
> A VOTE FOR ELLE IS A VOTE FOR YOUR
>   SOCIAL LIFE.
> KEEP SCHOOL DANCES ALIVE!
> DON'T KILL THE HOMECOMING DANCE—
>   VOTE ELLE.
> ELLE FOR PRESIDENT: A DATE FOR EVERY
>   STUDENT, EVERY DANCE, GUARANTEED!

Finally, after considering each slogan for what seemed like hours, the two girls decided to go with something short and sweet. Two words; one simple message: VOTE BLONDE.

"Elle! Elle! She's your girl! Blaylock's just a giant pill! Vo-o-ote *Elle!"*

The cheerleadering squad jumped up and down and shook their pom-poms as they sprinted through the halls the next day. Elle and Laurette hung campaign posters and handed out buttons that said: VOTE BLONDE in bright pink letters. Elle frowned when she heard the cheerleaders' chant.

"I want them to promote me, not insult Curt," she said. "No mudslinging."

"Calling him a pill isn't so terrible," Laurette said. "I think he can handle it. He might even consider it a compliment."

"This could be a problem, you know," Chessie said as she took one of Elle's Vote Blonde buttons. "What if Curt suddenly decides to dye his hair?"

"We'll deal with that when the time comes," Laurette said.

"If he goes blond, I'll pull a counteroffensive and go red," Elle said.

Chessie stepped back to assess Elle's potential as a redhead. "No, I'm not seeing that. Brown, maybe . . ."

"Whatever," Laurette said. "Somehow, I'm not too worried about Elle's hair color."

"You should be," Chessie said. "It's getting a little dishwatery."

Elle's hand flew to her hair. "It must be time for a touch-up." She was usually careful about keeping up with her salon appointments. Bibi Barbosa, her manicurist and hairstylist, was like a therapist to her.

Alicia Berg fingered a campaign button. "What's going on?" she asked. "You're running for president?"

"Is this a joke?" Kyra Holmbeck said.

"It's for real," Elle said.

"Really?" Alicia said.

"Really," Elle said.

"Ha-ha. That's funny, Elle," Kyra said.

"I'm serious," Elle said.

"Is she?" Alicia asked Laurette.

"Totally," Laurette said.

"You guys, stop kidding around," Kyra said.

"Yeah, we get the joke," Alicia said.

"Do you think we'd go to all this trouble just to make a lame joke?" Laurette said.

Alicia and Kyra looked at the posters and buttons and Elle's T-shirt, which had a picture of her face silk-screened on it with the words *Vote Blonde* in pink.

"It is a lot of work for a joke," Alicia said.

"And I guess it really isn't that funny," Kyra said. "Once you've gotten it."

"No, wait, it is," Alicia said. "I just pictured Elle leading a student senate meeting. Go ahead, picture it, Kyra. You'll die!"

Kyra shut her eyes as if she were imagining Elle as president. Then she cracked up. "You're right! That's hilarious!"

"Stop it, you guys," Elle said. But Kyra and Alicia stumbled laughing down the hall, stopping everyone they met and saying, "Wait until you see the big joke Elle's got going!"

Elle looked at Laurette, who shrugged. "They're idiots," Laurette said.

David Reese, a small, cute boy in Elle's class, and his taller friend, Jake Bott, stopped to read one of her posters. "You're running for president?" David asked.

"That's what it says on the poster," Laurette said. "Right there in pink letters. Why does everyone keep asking us that?"

"Just checking," David said. "You've got my vote, Elle."

"Thanks, David."

"If you'll go out with me."

"Well, I can't," Elle said. "I've got a boyfriend."

"Oh. Okay," David said.

"But you'll still vote for me, won't you?" Elle asked.

David shrugged. "I don't know. I might not bother to vote. What difference does it make, anyway?"

"Blaylock was an okay president," Jake said. "I'll probably just vote for him again."

"What did he do that was so good?" Laurette asked.

"I don't know," Jake said. "What does the school president do, anyway?"

"Lots of things," Elle said. "Curt wants to abolish all dances. Did you know that?"

"Eh," Jake said. "I don't really care."

"Me, neither," David said.

"But I can get you a date for every school dance," Elle said, pointing to the slogan on her poster.

"I won't need a date if there aren't any dances," Jake said. "It would make my life a lot easier."

"Will *you* be my date at the dance?" David asked Elle.

"David, I already told you—"

"Some campaign promise," David said. "What do I care if you get me a date if she's not the one I want to go with? I could do that myself."

"Yeah, it's better to have no dance at all," Jake said.

"Even the Homecoming Dance?" Chessie said.

"The Homecoming Dance?" Jake said. "Who cares about that?"

"I hate to dance anyway," David said as he turned away.

"This isn't going very well," Elle said, watching David and Jake walk down the hall.

"Elle, you're doomed," Chessie said. "I'm saying that out of love."

"We need a new approach," Laurette said. "Something that will grab them. An issue that really matters to them."

"But what?" Elle said. "Nothing matters to them."

"There's got to be something," Laurette said.

"Oh, my God." Chessie gripped Elle's wrist until her hand turned white. "It's Chris Rodriguez!" She flashed her teeth in Elle's face. "Do I have anything in my teeth? Is my lip gloss still on?"

"You're fine," Elle said. So Chessie liked Chris. It figured. Since Hunter had graduated, Chris had been promoted to chief hottie.

"Why is Delilah Howe with him?" Chessie whispered. "Are they going out?"

"I don't know," Elle whispered back.

"You're running for president?" Delilah and Chris asked, pointing at Elle's poster. "*Vote Blonde.* That's hilarious!" Chris said.

"There's nothing funny about it," Elle said. "Curt Blaylock wants to make changes that could ruin the whole school."

"You mean the dance thing? Yawn," Delilah said.

"It's hard to get too worked up about it," Chris said.

"Even about Homecoming, Chris?" Chessie said. "Don't you think the Homecoming Dance is wonderful? With the crowns, and everyone cheering for the King and Queen, and then they dance together, and then they kiss—"

"Chris is going to be the Homecoming King," Delilah said, pinching him playfully. It was hard to tell if she was serious or joking.

"I am not," Chris said.

"Yes, you are," Delilah said. "I'm going to nominate him. I want to see how he looks with a crown on his head."

"You'd look great, Chris," Chessie said.

"If it happens, it happens," Chris said.

"Then you'll vote for me?" Elle said. "So you can preside over the Homecoming Dance?"

Chris shrugged. "I don't know. There's the Homecoming game, too. And the halftime ceremony. That's probably enough Homecoming junk for one day."

"He didn't have a very good time at the last dance he went to," Delilah said. "Did you, Chris?"

"Why?" Elle asked. "What happened?"

"Nothing," Chris said.

"His girlfriend, Jessica, dumped him," Delilah said. "Right there at the dance. She spent the rest of the night slow-dancing with John Fourier."

"Jessica McMartin?" Elle said. "She's a cheerleader."

"That's right." Delilah leaned toward Elle and stage-whispered, "It's a painful memory. He doesn't like to think about it."

"That's not true," Chris said. "I'm totally over Jessica."

"They haven't spoken since that night," Delilah said.

"That's a shame," Elle said.

"No, it's good," Chessie said. "Jessica's really not your type anyway, Chris."

"Whatever," Chris said. "I'm not that big on dances."

Elle was discouraged, but she never gave up.

She pressed one of her Vote Blonde buttons into Chris's palm. "I still hope you'll vote for me."

"Maybe," Chris said. "If I get around to it."

"It's not that we don't like you," Delilah said.

"Yeah, you seem sweet," Chris said.

"You're just not presidential material," Delilah said.

"I am too," Elle said.

They walked away, laughing like all the others.

"Don't worry, Elle," Laurette said. "You are presidential material. And by the time the election comes, everybody will know it."

"Okay," Elle said. "But how can we convince them?"

As she said those words, an answer came to her: Bibi.

Chapter 4

"DO YOU think it's my hair?" Elle asked. "Should I get rid of the blonde?"

She was sitting in Bibi Barbosa's chair at the Pamperella Salon. Elle visited Bibi as often as she could for manicures and advice. This, however, was an emergency. Underdog jumped off her lap to play with Bibi's dog, Kitty, who was his mother.

"Maybe people would take me more seriously if I were a brunette," Elle said.

"No," Bibi said. "Don't you touch that hair. This shade of vanilla blonde is perfect for you. Go a smidgen lighter or darker and you won't win Miss Clairol, let alone school president. You're a blonde through and through. You've got to get those kids to accept you as you are."

"It just seems like people don't think of me as someone who can be a leader."

"That's ridiculous. You already are a leader—a cheerleader. And not just any cheerleader, but the captain. If that's not leadership, Dallas is the capital of Sweden. Do people realize how hard it is to get twelve self-absorbed social princesses to line up and do as they're told? You have to be as tough as a marine corps sergeant."

"You're right," Elle said. "Being captain of the squad is not easy. Even Chloe didn't want the job."

"So you let those kids know it. However . . ." She spun Elle's chair around for a better look at the total package. "There are a few things you could do to look more presidential. Are you with me?"

"Always," Elle said.

"Okay. Step one: makeup. More conservative, toned down. Easy on the eyeliner."

"Check," Elle said.

"Step two: hair. Keep the color, but cut it a little more blunt, maybe put it up in a French twist for debates and things like that. What do you think?"

"Sounds good."

"Step three: clothes. I'm seeing solid colors, jackets. Watch the bold prints. Nothing too girly or flowery. And lots of red. Stay away from pink."

"What?" Elle wailed. "But pink is my favorite color."

"I know, honey." Bibi patted her on the shoulder. "But it's only temporary, till you're elected. After that you can go back to pink, lace, frills, ruffles, the whole bit. Are you in?"

"I'm in," Elle said. She'd just gotten used to wearing sexy designer clothes, but now she'd have to start dressing like somebody's mother. Still, if it helped her campaign, it would be worth it.

Bibi washed her hair, then started tweaking the cut. "You don't want to change yourself too much, you know," she said. "People might make fun of you now, for running for office, but that's just because they're not used to thinking of you that way. How much time do you have until the election?"

"A month and a half," Elle said.

"Good," Bibi said. "You stay in their faces, and by election day, they'll take you seriously. At the very least. I think you can win this thing."

"You do?" Elle wanted to jump up and hug her, but Bibi was holding the scissors very close to her face. "Thank you, Bibi! You always make me feel better."

"It's going to take some work," Bibi warned. "I

didn't say you wouldn't have to work for it."

"I know."

"But you've never been lazy, so I'm not worried about that," Bibi said. "Tilt your head down. I'm having a vision of a President Elle with wispy bangs."

Elle tilted her head.

"Is anyone else running besides you and this Curt guy?" Bibi asked.

"Just Merlin Jones," Elle said. "But he runs for everything. And he never wins."

"You watch out for him," Bibi said. "He could be your spoiler."

"What do you mean?" Elle asked. "Hardly anybody even likes him. I've actually thought about voting for him myself, just to boost his self-esteem."

"Don't you do that! If Curt is smart, he could use Merlin to form an anti-Elle coalition. They could team up their votes and beat you that way."

"Really? But Merlin's votes only add up to maybe two, if you count him and my pity vote."

"Not if Curt uses him wisely," Bibi said. "I don't know exactly what he'd do. All I'm saying is, watch your back."

"Okay, Bibi," Elle said. "I will."

★ ★ ★

"Thank you, Beverly Hills High Marching Band, for that rousing rendition of the theme from *Starship Troopers*. Let's give them all a big hand!" Ms. Mikulski, the school principal, waved her arm at the marching band, but very little applause came. Tuba player Merlin Jones and French horn player Sidney Ugman stood in the front row, waiting. It was a morning assembly a few days after Elle had announced her candidacy.

"Ugh," Laurette groaned. "Isn't it a little early in the day to subject us to that?"

"Sounds like the members of the marching band didn't get much practice over the summer," Elle said. "I'll have to speak to Sidney about it." Which she knew she'd put off, because the last thing she wanted to do was speak to Sidney Ugman about anything.

"And now for today's announcements," Ms. Mikulski said. "The Killer Bees have their first football game of the season this afternoon against archrivals Santa Monica—everybody, come on out! We have a good team this year, and with our new and improved school spirit, thanks to an excellent cheerleading squad and an entertaining marching band, you're sure to have a good time. The big Homecoming game is only a few weeks away, so the team needs your support.

"Speaking of Homecoming, there are two important elections coming up: Homecoming King and Queen, and student body president. The candidates for Homecoming Royalty will be announced next week. For president, the nominations are in, and here are the candidates: Curt Blaylock, Merlin Jones, and Elle Woods."

There was tepid applause. "We will have two candidates' debates. The first will be here in the auditorium, one week from today. The second will take place the week of the election. Would the candidates please come up on stage?"

Elle scrambled past the knees of her classmates and up the aisle to join Merlin on the stage. Curt stood off to the side for a minute while his campaign manager, Maggie Licht, whispered in his ear. Maggie was pinched-looking and wore pointy glasses and extra–narrow penny loafers with dimes in the penny slots. She was never without her cell phone. Suzanne Marconi, the student treasurer, stood quietly nearby. Suzanne was tall and gawky. It was hard to tell what her face looked like, because she mostly hid behind a curtain of brown hair.

"Curt? Whenever you're ready," Ms. Mikulski said.

Curt nodded and went to stand next to Elle on

the stage, a smug look on his face.

"Do any of you have anything you want to say to announce your candidacies?" Ms. Mikulski asked.

Curt stepped forward. The part in his hair was like a superstraight white laser beam cutting a line through his head. He cleared his throat.

"I would like to say that I welcome my fellow candidates to the fray. Competition is good: that's the American way. I wouldn't want to win the election without a challenge, even if the challengers are an airhead and a geek. So, thanks, Merlin and Elle, for sacrificing yourselves so that I may be a better leader. Last year the slogan that got me elected by a seventy percent margin was *Blaylock, a Born Leader.* My slogan for this campaign will be: *I hate dances. You hate dances. Let Curt get rid of them for you.* Or something like that. I might tweak it a little. It doesn't make a whole lot of difference, does it? I'm a shoo-in. Thank you."

Maggie cheered, whistled, and clapped loudly. She was pretty much the only one. Curt bowed slightly and stepped back to let Elle and Merlin take their turns. Elle hadn't expected this; she hadn't prepared a speech and didn't know what to say. She glanced at Merlin, who looked just as uncomfortable as she was.

"Elle? Merlin?" Ms. Mikulski prompted. "Any words?"

"Go ahead," he whispered to her.

"You first," she whispered back. She gave him a gentle poke in the back. He squeaked and hopped forward. Now he had to say something.

"Um, I haven't come up with a slogan yet," he said. "But I was thinking something like *Merlin, the Man with the Band*. That's what I doodled on my notebook last night, anyway. Thanks."

An anonymous voice from the crowd shouted, "Nerd!"

As if to acknowledge his nerd status, Merlin gave a little toot on his tuba. He made way for Elle, who was shaking with nervousness. She stepped forward.

"Thank you," she said. The microphone squealed. "I like dances. Dances are awesome! What kind of grinch wants to get rid of them?"

"Dances suck!" somebody yelled.

"Cheerleader!" another voice shouted. "Get some brains!"

"Just because I'm a cheerleader doesn't mean I don't have brains," Elle said.

"Rah-rah, blondie!"

The crowd began to get restless. Elle could

sense it, so she cut it short.

"Here's my slogan: *A Date for Every Student to Every Dance, Guaranteed!*"

The students laughed. "What's it going to be— you and every guy in school?" a boy shouted. "That should be good."

Elle turned red and stepped away from the microphone. She wanted to run off the stage in tears, but she knew that wouldn't be very presidential of her.

"Thank you, candidates," Ms. Mikulski said. "Homecoming will take place the day after the presidential election, so we have decided to combine the two elections to save time. Have a good school day, and don't forget about the football team's season opener this afternoon!"

The students dispersed for their first-period classes. Elle found Laurette and Chessie waiting for her as she left the stage.

Maggie was alternating between talking to Curt and talking to someone else on her cell. "Looks like I'm up against Pinch-face in a battle of the campaign managers," Laurette said.

"That's not very nice," Elle said. "Remember, Laurette, no mudslinging."

"I wasn't mudslinging," Laurette said. "She does

have a very pinched face."

Elle couldn't argue with that. "What a disaster."

"It wasn't so bad," Laurette said, "but we do have a few things to work on."

"What difference does it make?" Chessie said. "Nobody cares about the stupid election anyway."

"I care," Elle said.

"Of course you do," Chessie said. "I'm just saying you shouldn't feel bad for making a ginormous fool of yourself in front of the whole school, because by lunchtime everyone will have forgotten all about it."

"Thanks, Chessie," Elle said.

"Yeah, Chessie," Laurette said. "You're helpful and uplifting as always."

"I try," Chessie said.

Chapter 5

"HALFTIME! AND the score is Beverly Hills 10, Santa Monica 7." Red Ripkin, the new school sports announcer, was only a freshman, but he was already pretty good. He was one of those guys who gave a running commentary on everything, as if he'd been born in front of a microphone.

"Stay glued to your seats, folks! We've got a great halftime show featuring the Beverly Hills High Marching Band and the fabulous Beverly Hills cheerleaders!"

The first football game of the season was going well. The Bees looked good and the crowd was happy. Red started the cheerleaders' music and the squad went out on the field to do their thing, with

Elle leading the way as captain.

"Ready? Let's go!" And they started dancing and flipping and flying through the air.

> *Killer Bees got the moves! Killer Bees know the grooves! They dance in the end zone; dance, dance, dance! By now it should be evident Elle Woods will be our president. Vote blonde, yeah! Go, Elle!*

"Yay! Vote for Elle!" the cheerleaders shouted as they broke up.

"Hey," Merlin said to Elle as she passed him on the sidelines. "You can't do that! You're using the cheerleading squad to promote your campaign!"

Laurette stepped in, playing the pit bull. "Where does it say she can't do that?" she asked Merlin. "I never saw a rule against it."

"I just think it's wrong, that's all," Merlin sniffed.

The marching band took the field, playing a song from *Camelot*. They formed the shape of a wizard's hat while they played, then morphed into letters spelling the word MERLIN.

"Huh," Elle said. "Looks like he had the same idea we did."

"Hypocrite," Laurette said.

"Nice try, guys." Elle turned around to find Maggie Licht hovering nearby with a notebook in her arms and cell phone in her hand. "But you're crazy if you think this amateur stuff will get you votes. We're going the classy route—free underpants with I HEART CURT on the bottom."

"That *is* classy," Laurette said.

"Maybe you should forget about the election and concentrate on helping the football team win, like you're supposed to," Maggie said. "Curt is unbeatable. Get used to it." She turned and marched away. Her cell phone jingled. She flipped it open and started barking orders into it.

"Nobody is unbeatable!" Elle shouted after her. "Curt may be the president of the school, but he's not the king. Right, Laurette?"

Laurette was watching a commotion in the stands. Elle followed her gaze. Curt was walking through the home crowd, passing out free underpants and basking in the fans' approval.

"They love him," Elle said.

"They love free underwear, anyway," Laurette said.

"People love free stuff," Elle said. "We need to give them something, too—something they'll like better than buttons or even underwear."

"What could possibly be better than underwear?" Laurette asked.

"Lots of things," Elle said.

"Okay, but what?"

"I don't know," Elle said. "I have to think about it."

"My mama always used to say that the way to a man's heart is through his stomach," Zosia said after dinner that night.

"That works for me," Bernard said. "It's true for men *and* boys. The first girl I ever liked made the best brownies. . . ."

Elle bit into a warm, freshly baked sugar cookie—Bernard's specialty. "*Mmmm* . . . I think that old saying is true for girls, too. Our hearts and stomachs are totally connected. Even Underdog loves to be fed special treats; don't you, Underdog?"

She lifted him onto her lap. He licked the sugary crumbs from her hand, which she took as a yes.

"So it's official," Elle said. "The way to *anyone's* heart is through the stomach. That's how I'll get votes. I'll make something good to eat for the whole school."

"It can't hurt," Bernard said. "What are you going to make?"

"I don't know," Elle said. "Maybe Hunter will have an idea." She opened her cell and speed-dialed him.

"Hello?" he said in a whisper.

"Hunter?" Elle said. "Why are you whispering?"

"I'm in the library," he said.

"Oh," Elle said. "You're studying. Never mind. I'll call you later."

"Wait," Hunter whispered. "Don't go so fast. What are you doing?"

"Not much," she said. "Sitting in the kitchen, eating cookies with Bernard and Zosia."

"Sugar cookies?" Hunter asked. "Bernard's sugar cookies?"

"Yes," Elle said. "How did you know?"

"I've been dreaming of them for weeks," Hunter said. "I'd do almost anything for one of those cookies. They're like magic, those cookies."

"Interesting . . . I'll send some to you," Elle said.

"Did you want to ask me something?" Hunter said.

"You already answered my question," Elle said.

"I'll call you later," Hunter said.

Elle clicked off.

"What did he say?" Bernard asked.

"Cookies," Elle said. "These cookies, to be

exact." She took another one from the plate on the table. "Bernard, can I have your recipe?"

"Vote for Elle! Elle Woods for president!"

Elle and Laurette had called a meeting at cheerleading headquarters the next morning, and all the girls had volunteered to help with the baking. They decided on heart-shaped sugar cookies with "Vote Blonde" written on them in silver icing. By the next day they had made boxes and boxes of them. Elle made sure to send Hunter a tin of them.

Elle, Laurette, Chessie, and the other cheerleaders passed out their cookies in the school hallways after lunch. Kids lined up to take them.

"Thanks," one boy said. "My mom forgot to pack me a dessert today."

"You're welcome," Laurette said. "Don't forget to vote for Elle on election day."

"I love homemade cookies," another boy said. "My mom never bakes anymore." He took a bite. "Mmmm . . . I'll never forget this."

"That's the idea," Elle said.

"Don't forget to read the cookie before you eat it," Laurette said. "Vote for Elle!"

Elle surveyed the crowd with satisfaction. The cookie plan seemed to be working. People were really taking notice of her as a candidate.

Suddenly there was a low roar, as if someone were driving a motorcycle through the hall.

"What is that?" Elle asked.

A giant red-white-and-blue three-layer cake rolled down the hallway on a motorized cart. Across the sides, in sparkling gold letters, was written "Reelect Curt," and on top was a life-size cardboard cutout of Curt himself.

"Oh, my God," Laurette murmured.

The cake rumbled to a stop. Kids fled Elle's cookie trays and ran to the cake to see what was up.

An amplified voice came from inside the cake. *"Students of Beverly Hills! Curt Blaylock cares about you! He's willing to do anything to get your vote—and he'll prove it!"*

The cake rumbled some more, and Curt burst out of the top like a stripper at a bachelor party. "Got that after-lunch sugar jones? Chocolate cupcakes for everyone!" he shouted.

The kids screamed for joy and rushed up to get their free cupcakes.

"They're from Cupcake Castle, the best bakery in Beverly Hills," Curt said.

"Wait!" Elle shouted. "I've got homemade cookies! Made with heart and tender loving care! Loving care for you, the students of Beverly Hills!"

Her pleas couldn't be heard above the clamor over Curt's giant cake. Elle and her team were deserted. No one cared about cookies anymore. Cupcakes beat them by a mile.

"I don't believe this," Elle said. "It's like he had the same idea I did, only better."

"Way better," P.J. said.

The whole school, it seemed, mobbed Curt. "Take as many as you want!" he told them. "I don't want anything in return. Oh, except for your vote. But how hard is that? You were going to vote for me anyway, right?"

"Listen!" Chessie ran over to Elle with one of Curt's cupcakes. Baked into the center was a tiny plastic toy radio with a computer chip in it. When pressed, it made a tinny rock song play. The chorus went: *Curt Blaylock, the smartest dude who ever ran for president of any school. He's smart, he's cool. Vote Curt!*

"That's just evil," Laurette said.

"Each cupcake plays one of the Curt songs," Chessie said. "There's a hip-hop version, a pop version, an emo version, an opera version, even an Irish jig . . ."

Elle clutched her box of homemade sugar

cookies, which somehow seemed pathetic compared to Curt's cupcakes.

"He's amazing," Chessie said. "He's so smart. He can do anything!"

"Hey," Elle said.

"Oh, but I'm still totally voting for you, Elle," Chessie said. "Of course!"

"Don't worry about it, Elle," P.J. said. "Just because people want free cupcakes and stuff doesn't mean they'll vote for Curt. After all, you get the cupcakes whether you vote for him or not, so why bother?"

"Curt wouldn't do this if he didn't think it would get him votes," Laurette said. "He's smarter than that."

"It's funny that we both brought treats on the same day," Elle said, thinking out loud. "As if we had the same thought at the same time. What a coincidence."

"I don't think it's all that funny," Laurette said. "And I'm not so sure it's a coincidence."

"What else could it be?" Elle said.

Laurette shrugged.

"This campaign isn't over yet," Elle said. "We'll just have to try harder."

"How can we compete with this?" Laurette

asked. The students in the mob around the giant cake had worked themselves into a chocolate frenzy.

"I don't know," Elle said. "Maybe we'll try a different tack. Time to do a little research—Elle style."

Chapter 6

THAT NIGHT Elle started a political movie marathon, watching everything from *Citizen Kane* to *The Manchurian Candidate*. Zosia, Bernard, and Laurette passed through her room at various times to watch with her.

"Pull up a chair," Elle said to Laurette. She was sitting in her favorite pink velour beanbag chair, with Underdog in her lap.

Laurette chose a white one and sat down. "Which movies do you like best?"

"So far I like *All the President's Men* and *The Candidate*," Elle said. "I'm not sure why."

"I'll tell you why," Zosia said. She sat in a yellow beanbag chair, nibbling on popcorn. "They both star Robert Redford. Talk about gorgeous."

"Maybe that's it," Elle said. "Also, he's blond. Look, Laurette. In *The Candidate* he's blond and idealistic, and everyone says he has no chance of winning. Just like me! But he wins the election. Maybe I should model myself on him."

"Okay, sure," Laurette said. "But by the end of the campaign he loses his idealism and becomes a cynical wheeler-dealer."

"So?" Elle said. "We'll just skip that part."

"But the point of the movie is that you can't skip that part," Laurette said. "It's an inevitable part of the political process."

"Movies aren't always right, you know," Elle said. "You have to take what you need from them and leave the rest."

"Elle knows what she's talking about," Zosia said. "She watches a lot of movies."

Underdog jumped off Elle's lap and pushed his nose into the bowl of popcorn.

"Underdog, no!" Elle pulled him away. "You don't want to get a tummy ache."

Laurette reached for the popcorn bowl, then set it back down. "Ewww, dog germs."

"Don't worry, it's just Underdog germs," Elle said. "He's very clean. He licks my face all the time, and nothing bad ever happens to me."

"Still," Laurette said, "I don't have as much immunity as you do."

Zosia got to her feet and picked up the bowl. "I'll get some more popcorn," she said, "and a clean bowl."

"Thanks, Zosia!" Elle called as Zosia left for the kitchen. She paused the movie until Zosia got back.

"Underdog, la-la-la-la . . ." Laurette sang the theme from the old cartoon show. *"Underdog. Underdog!"*

Suddenly, her dog's name took on a new meaning for Elle. A political meaning. And it gave her an idea.

"That's it!" Elle cried. "Underdog!"

"What about him?" Laurette said. "We're not going to give a free dog to every kid in school, are we?"

"No," Elle said. "I'm talking about his name. We'll play the *underdog.*"

Zosia returned with a tray holding a big bowl of fresh popcorn and three mugs of hot chocolate. "What did I miss?"

Elle repeated her idea.

"I don't get it," Zosia said.

"In *The Candidate*, people don't take Robert

Redford seriously," Elle says. "He's the underdog. So he uses that to his advantage. He makes his opponent think he has the election all wrapped up, that he doesn't have to work too hard. Then he slips under the radar—"

"Curt is already totally complacent," Laurette said.

"And we'll keep him that way," Elle said. "Make him think we have no idea what we're doing."

"But he's right—you *don't* have any idea what you're doing," Zosia said.

"And that's good," Elle said.

"It is?" Laurette said.

"Didn't you hear what I just said?" Elle said. "That's my new plan."

"I don't get it," Laurette said.

"I'll explain it to the cheerleaders tomorrow," Elle said. "The key is, Curt can't know what we're really up to."

"But what *are* we up to?"

"We're acting dumb."

"That's the plan?" Laurette said.

"So far," Elle said.

"As your campaign manager, I officially declare a headache," Laurette said. "Let's meet at HQ tomorrow and figure this out."

"HQ?" Zosia asked. "What's that?"

"Elle Woods for President Campaign Head-quarters," Laurette explained, "in the cheerleading practice room."

"It's the best place to talk without being over-heard," Elle said. "No one is allowed in there but cheerleaders."

"And they're all so trustworthy," Laurette said sarcastically.

"They are," Elle said.

"I'm with Laurette," Zosia said. "Put a gang of pretty girls together in a room and you're just ask-ing for trouble."

"We're the underdogs, right?" Elle told the room full of cheerleaders just before practice the next day. "So let's take advantage of it. Here's my plan. Campaign manager?"

Laurette stepped up to explain the plan, which she had finally managed to understand. Elle was the idea person; it was Laurette's job to put the ideas into practice, which wasn't always easy.

"People are pretty apathetic about this election already," Laurette said. "They want to take the cup-cakes and run. Your job is to make them even more bored with it. Go around talking about how Curt is a sure thing and doesn't need your vote.

Then nobody will bother to vote for him. On election day, we'll all vote for Elle. That's fifteen votes right there. If nobody else votes for Curt—because, remember, they think he doesn't need their vote—Elle will win."

"That's pretty risky," P.J. said.

"But it might work," Chloe said. "Beverly kids are just that apathetic. How did you ever think of it?"

"It was inspired by a Robert Redford movie, and my dog," Elle said.

"Elle, your mind is so full of junk," Chessie said. "I mean that in the best possible way."

"Remember: Curt is a shoo-in, and no one should bother to vote," Laurette said. "Voting is totally uncool. Got it?"

"Got it," the cheerleaders said in unison.

"Good," Laurette said. "Now get out there and spread the word. Fly, my pretties, fly!"

"But we have practice now," Chessie said.

"Oh. Right," Laurette said. "Tomorrow, then."

From: hperry
To: elliebelly
Re: thank u
Date: Thurs 25 Sept 8:03 PM

thanks for the sugar cookies, elle! mmmm! If I could just keep my suite mates from eating them all! u r so thoughtful, sweeter than bernard's cookies . . .

how's the campaign going? did the cookies help?

hunter

From: elliebelly
To: hperry
Re: thank u
Date: Thurs 25 Sept 9:10 PM

the cookies didn't work. but i have a new plan now. it involves robert redford. we're combining my weakness (low expectations) with the voters' weakness (low interest in the election). two minuses equal a plus, right? hope i've got my algebra straight.

i'll send you more cookies tomorrow. we've got plenty left over. so your suite mates can have all they want!

xxxxoooolovelovelovelove,

elle

Chapter 7

"HALLOWEEN ALREADY?" Elle said. "It feels as if school just started." She and Laurette sat outside in the school courtyard, eating their sandwiches in the warm southern California sun.

"It's coming up," Laurette said. "They're already building the Haunted House."

"I love the Haunted House," Elle said.

The Haunted House was set up every Halloween in the gym. Students decorated it with spooky cobwebs, glow-in-the dark paint, and icky mystery goos. They dressed up as ghosts and ghouls and witches and wandered through the house, jumping out and shouting, "Boo!" They charged admission and gave the money to a children's charity.

Elle smelled bologna and turned to see Sidney Ugman lurking behind her.

"What are you going to be for Halloween this year?" he asked.

"I don't know yet," Elle said. "I've been so focused on the election I haven't thought about it."

"You know, Elle," Sidney said, "if you need help getting ready for the big debate, I'm your man. I was on the debate team last year."

"Thanks, Sidney," Elle said. It was time to begin to implement her plan: Project Underdog. "But I'm not going to bother to prep for the debate. Curt's a lock. Why fight it?"

"Well, the polls do show him in the lead," Sidney said, "but you've got a few weeks to turn it around. Don't give up so easily, Elle."

"You know me," Elle said. "I'm a big quitter."

Elle was enjoying this; she thought of herself as an actress playing a role. She was going to prep for the debate, but she wanted expectations to be low. That way, when she steamrollered over Curt and Merlin with her whip–smart speaking style (which she would somehow acquire in the next three weeks), everyone would be totally wowed.

Pretending she wasn't prepping for the debate had the added advantage of keeping Sidney at bay.

"Aren't you voting for Merlin anyway?" Elle said. "He's your bandmate, after all."

"I could never vote against you, Elle," Sidney said. He sat down on the bench beside her.

Elle swallowed her last bite of sandwich and stood up.

"Sorry, we have to go," she told him, with a glance at Laurette.

Sidney stood up again. "I'll come with you."

"You can't," Laurette said. "Girl business."

"Oh. Okay. Bye, Elle," Sidney said.

Elle and Laurette went inside the school building. The walls were plastered with Vote Curt posters. Curt and Maggie put up more every day, covering Elle's posters with theirs and playing right into her hands. . . .

Kyra and David stopped Elle in the hall. "I hear your campaign is really picking up steam," Kyra said.

"What? No it isn't," Elle said. "It's limping along. Dying. Curt is unbeatable. Don't bother to vote."

"That's not what I heard," David said. "Curt told me he's way behind and needs lots of votes to beat you."

"He did?" Elle was confused. How could the polls show him way ahead, when he was telling everybody that his campaign—

Wait a minute, she thought.

"I think we've got another cupcake situation," Laurette said. "Another so-called coincidence."

"Let's go," Elle said.

She and Laurette ran down the hall until they came to the main lobby and the big central bulletin board. Maggie stood on a ladder, tearing Curt's posters down.

"Maggie, what are you doing?" Elle asked. She was eye to toe with Maggie's extra–narrow dime loafers.

"These posters are just wasting space," Maggie said. "Curt doesn't have a chance against you, Elle. How can a regular guy like him beat a cute blonde cheerleader?"

"What?" Elle was flabbergasted. Where was this coming from?

"I told you," Laurette said. "'Coincidence.'"

"Are you dropping out of the race?" Elle asked Maggie.

"No," Maggie said. "We're just toning it down. Why waste our energy on a losing proposition?"

"But you can't," Elle said. "You're the front-runner. . . ."

"Not anymore," Maggie said. "You've got a

whole political machine working for you. The Cheerleader Party."

"It's not a political machine," Elle said. "It's just a rah-rah team."

"Yeah—rah-rah for Elle," Maggie said. "Face it, Elle. You're the Establishment. Fight the power!"

"I'm the Establishment?" Elle said. "But Curt is already school president!"

"It's so like you Establishment types to expect everything to make sense," Maggie said. Her cell phone rang, and she answered it.

Elle and Laurette wandered away down the hall.

"What is she talking about? I don't understand," Elle said.

"Curt is undermining our underdog strategy," Laurette said. "They must think that if they make themselves look like losers, they can rally the voters and win. They're trying to steal the sympathy vote from us. Our plan is backfiring."

"This is so confusing," Elle said. "How did he know what our plan was in the first place? We just started it today."

"Someone told him about it," Laurette said.

"But who would do that?" Elle said. "No one knew about it except the cheerleaders. And they would never betray me. The squad is faithful and loyal. You heard the oath."

"I don't know," Laurette said. "Somehow Curt and Maggie keep figuring out our strategies before we can make them work. And now it looks like we need a new plan. Again."

Elle stopped at her locker to get her history textbook. She found a note taped to the door. "Look at this." She showed the folded piece of paper to Laurette.

"Open it."

Ellie quickly unfolded the note. *"I have some information you need,"* she read. *"Meet me inside the Haunted House today at four. Come alone."*

It had been typed on a computer and printed out, so there was no handwriting to decipher. And it wasn't signed.

"Who could have written this?" Elle asked.

"I don't know," Laurette said. "Are you going to go?"

"Of course I am," Elle said. "Maybe we'll find out how Curt is getting all our secrets."

"I'll come with you," Laurette said.

"No," Elle said. "It says to come alone. I don't want to do anything to mess this up."

Chapter 8

"HELLO? IS anyone here?" Elle said.

Four o'clock had come at last. The Haunted House was almost finished, but it wasn't open to the public yet. The gym was unrecognizable, except for the telltale sweaty-socks smell that nothing seemed to get rid of. It was dark inside. There was no sign of anyone around.

Suddenly, a red light flashed over the door of the Haunted House. The spooky noises—a running recorded loop of screams, howls, boos, evil laughs, and scary organ music—started up. Elle knew it was just for fun, but she still felt jittery. Who was waiting here for her? What did they want to tell her?

Welcome. On the recording a deep, ghostly voice boomed. *Step inside . . . if you dare. . . . Bwa-ha-ha-ha-ha!* There was a scream, and a mechanized bat flapped past Elle's head and disappeared through a gabled cardboard window.

She stepped through the front door and found herself in a long, dark passageway. "Hello? Mysterious note-writer? Are you here?"

"Keep walking," a voice said.

Elle couldn't tell if it was a boy's voice or a girl's, because the speaker was using one of those electronic voice-changing devices that makes everyone sound like a serial killer. It was a good thing Elle had seen *Scream*, or she might not have known that.

"I'm in the Chamber of Horrors."

"Who are you?" Elle asked.

"Just a little farther," the voice said.

Elle walked through the house until she came to a dark room full of tombstones and coffins.

"Stay where you are," the voice said.

Elle stopped.

"Don't come any closer," the voice said.

"But I want to see the rest of the house," Elle said. *It's not a ghost, it's just a person*, she told herself, to keep calm.

"You can see it later," the voice said. "Afterward."

"After what?" Elle asked. The voice said nothing. At the other end of the room Elle could see a white blob. She peered through the darkness, trying to get a better look. It was someone dressed as a ghost, in a white sheet.

"Are you the person who wrote me the note?" Elle asked.

"Yes," the ghost said.

"Who are you?" Elle asked.

"Never mind," the ghost said. "Call me Deep Ghost."

"Just like in *All the President's Men!*" Elle said. "I saw that movie. The reporters meet with an anonymous tipster called Deep Throat."

"Duh, I already knew that," the ghost said. It sounded funny to hear a ghost say, "Duh," in a serial-killer voice. "That's why I chose to be called Deep Ghost."

"What information do you have?" Elle asked.

"You're in trouble," the ghost said.

"I'm in danger?" Elle asked.

"Not danger. Did I say danger?"

"You said something like that," Elle said.

"I didn't say danger. I said you're in trouble," the ghost said. "Your campaign is in trouble. I can't name names. But someone is working against you, with inside information."

Someone working against her? From the inside? So that was how Curt could anticipate every move she made. But who would do that to her?

"Who is it?" Elle asked. She couldn't imagine anyone she knew doing anything so underhanded.

"I just told you, I can't name names," the ghost said.

"So, what good are you?" Elle asked.

"I thought you should know," the ghost said. "I don't have all the facts yet. When I can tell you more, I will. Go away now. I'll contact you."

The ghost turned and disappeared into the shadows. Elle tried to follow, but then the ghost jumped out of nowhere and yelled, "Boo!"

Elle screamed and jumped back.

"Don't follow me!" the ghost roared. "Don't try to figure out who I am, or I won't help you!"

"Okay, okay," Elle said. "*Sheesh*, what a cranky ghost!"

"It's a mystery," Laurette said. "Two mysteries, really: who is the ghost, and who is the leak?"

"I don't know," Elle said, "but we'll have to be more careful who we tell our plans to from now on. Cheerleaders only."

"But we were telling our plans to cheerleaders only before," Laurette said. "Maybe one of the cheerleaders is the leak."

"How could that be?" Elle said. "What about the Cheerleader's Oath?"

"What about it?" Laurette said. "Maybe some cheerleaders don't take the oath as seriously as you do."

"That's impossible," Elle said. "A cheerleader's a cheerleader, through and through. We take everything about it seriously."

"Even those Killer Bee headbands you wear sometimes?" Laurette said. "With the fuzzy bee antennae sticking up from your heads?"

"Even those," Elle said solemnly.

"Today we'll announce the candidates for Homecoming King and Queen," the principal, Ms. Mikulski, said. "We'll have two voting tables on election day; one for president and one for Homecoming Royalty, so you can cast both votes at the same time."

It was the usual assembly chaos. Nobody was paying much attention. Elle caught Merlin slinging a jelly bean at the back of some girl's head. The girl turned around and scowled at him. It was

Maggie, and she didn't look too pleased.

"Guess that's his way of fighting the Curt Blaylock machine," Laurette whispered to Elle. "Shooting jelly beans at the campaign manager."

"Maybe he'll come after you next," Elle said.

"I hope so," Laurette said. "I could use a snack."

"The week before election day will be very exciting," Ms. Mikulski said. "We'll have a Homecoming Pageant, to give all the nominees a chance to show you why he or she should be Homecoming Royalty. And we'll also have the final presidential debate. So you'll have a lot to think about on the big day."

"I love the Homecoming Pageant," Elle said.

"Yeah, it's a chance to see people really make fools of themselves," Laurette said.

"We have only two candidates for Homecoming King," Ms. Mikulski said. "This honor is never as popular as I'd like it to be. What's the matter, boys? Don't you want to ride on a float surrounded by pretty girls? You get to wear a crown and a fake-fur robe."

There was a low grumble that sounded to Elle as if most of the boys didn't care much for that idea.

"The candidates are: Chris Rodriguez—" There was loud cheering, especially from the section of soccer players. Chris was a popular senior and star of the soccer team.

"—And Merlin Jones." This time there were boos. Merlin sank down in his seat.

"Merlin, aren't you running for president?" Ms. Mikulski asked.

"Yes," Merlin said.

"He really does run for everything," Elle said to Laurette.

"I don't know if you can run for both offices at the same time," Ms. Mikulski said. "I'll have to check the rules—"

"I already did," Merlin said. "There's no rule against it. You can be president, Homecoming King, head of every committee, and captain of the football team if you want to be."

"Well, okay," Ms. Mikulski said. "I'll check any-way, just to be sure."

"Go ahead," Merlin said, "if you want to waste your time."

"Talk about wasting time," Laurette said. "Who would ever vote for him for Homecoming King?"

"On to the girls," Ms. Mikulski said. "We have five candidates for Queen: Kyra Holmbeck, Anna Goodrow, Jessica McMasters, Chloe Gaitskill, and Chessie Morton. Good luck, girls."

"Whoa—did you see the look Chris just shot at Jessica?" Laurette said.

"I caught it," Elle said. Chris had given Jessica the evil eye, and she had sneered back at him. They still hadn't gotten over their breakup.

"I can't believe they're still mad at each other," Elle said. "They broke up months ago."

"Sometimes these things never heal," Laurette said. "What if Jessica wins? Will they have to go to the dance together?"

"I don't know what the rules are," Elle said. "But I hope Chloe or Chessie wins. It would be nice to have a cheerleader for Queen."

"Chloe's got a chance, but I can't imagine Chessie beating out any of those girls," Laurette said. "With her, you know, *problem*."

"She's been working on it," Elle said. "It's getting better."

But even Elle had to admit it was not by much.

Chessie's little problem was advanced clumsiness. Not just physically, though that was part of it. She was also clumsy about what she said and how she said it. She had a serious case of foot-in-mouth disease.

"All I'm saying is, Chessie would have to do something pretty spectacular to be chosen as

Homecoming Queen," Laurette said, "or else she'd have to cheat."

"Cheat? Not Chessie," Elle said.

Laurette shook her head. After all Chessie had done to Elle—trying to steal her boyfriend, helping her rival in a bikini contest, undermining her whenever she got the chance—Elle still refused to see anything but good in her. Laurette just didn't get it. But that was Elle's way.

"I need a new plan," Elle told Bibi during her weekly manicure. "Feeding the voters didn't work. Playing the underdog didn't work." She gave Underdog a little pat. "Curt outmaneuvered me every time."

"Something weird is definitely going on at that school of yours," Bibi said. "Sounds like your campaign is leakier than a balloon at a kitty cat's birthday party. Soak."

Elle dipped her left hand in the soaking dish while Bibi worked on the right hand.

"I've got to think of something Curt can't do," Elle said. "So it won't matter if there's a leak or not. Something I'm good at and he's not."

"I can name a lot of things like that," Bibi said. "Looking cute in a dress is one of them. Making friends easily is another."

"But that won't help my campaign," Elle said.

"What's your slogan again?" Bibi asked. "Something about dates for everybody?"

"'A date for every student, every dance,'" Elle said.

"Tough promise to keep," Bibi said.

"I know," Elle said.

"But think how powerful it would be if you could prove that you keep your promises," Bibi said. "What if you start making dates for people now—the kind of people who don't usually have dates? Dates for the Homecoming Dance."

"Good idea," Elle said. "If everyone's got dates for the dance, they're not going to want the dance to be canceled. So they'll vote for me. School dances will be saved, and everybody will be happy!"

"Sounds brilliant to me," Bibi said.

"You *are* brilliant," Elle said.

"No, *you're* brilliant. I'm just a sounding board. Okay, give me your left hand."

"Who should I start with?" Elle said. "Someone who's a real dating challenge. I need to impress everybody right away."

"How about Curt?" Bibi said. "He's never had a date, right? Isn't that his whole beef with dances in the first place? He'd be good to start with."

"He'd never go along with it," Elle said. "It would hurt his campaign. He really likes being president. Mostly, he likes bossing people around."

"That guy Merlin sounds like a pretty big loser," Bibi said. "What about him?"

"I saw him shoot a jelly bean at Maggie Licht today," Elle said. "She's Curt's campaign manager."

"Really?" Bibi said. "That means he likes her."

"Merlin likes Maggie? I don't know about that," Elle said.

"Sure," Bibi said. "Whenever a boy throws candy at a girl, that means he has a crush on her."

"Does it work the other way around?" Elle asked.

"Girls throwing candy at boys? Sure," Bibi said. "I'm telling you, it's foolproof."

"Huh," Elle said. "I didn't know that. The thing is, I'm not sure Maggie likes Merlin back. He *is* kind of the enemy. And she takes the campaign almost as seriously as Curt does."

"Did she throw the jelly bean back at him?" Bibi asked.

"I don't know," Elle said. "I wasn't paying that much attention."

"Next time, watch and see what she does," Bibi said. "He's sure to shoot candy at her again. If she throws it back at him, that means she likes him, too, no matter what she says."

"Where did you learn to be so smart?" Elle asked.

"In Texas, high school love rituals are a science," Bibi said. Bibi had been a teenage cheerleader in Texas before she moved to Los Angeles. "A required credit. We actually get a textbook about it in tenth grade. To help us decode what the heck is going on."

"Texas sounds so cool," Elle said.

Chapter 9

"FIRST OF all, I want to say congratulations to Chessie and Chloe," Elle said. "They're both running for Homecoming Queen. That means we could have a cheerleader as Homecoming Queen for the fifth year in a row. Yay, Chessie and Chloe!"

The cheerleaders applauded dutifully. Chloe threw an annoyed glance at Chessie, who was beaming with excitement.

"Now, back to *my* campaign," Elle said. "Plan C. Our slogan is 'A date for every student, every dance,' right? Right. So, to prove our word is good—and to get people excited about the Homecoming Dance—we'll start matching people up right now. Getting dates for the undatable. Think about the buzz! People won't be able to stop talking about the Homecoming Dance and the great dates they've got lined up. Sound good?"

"Yeah!" the cheerleaders cried simultaneously, excited about the idea.

Laurette stepped up. "Of course, some of you might have to make some sacrifices. . . ."

P.J. squinted suspiciously at her. "Sacrifices? What do you mean?"

"Not *sacrifices*," Elle said. "Just good deeds. For the cause!"

"I don't like the sound of this," Tamila said.

"It's no big deal," Elle said. "You might have to go to the dance with a guy who you wouldn't ordinarily pick. That's all."

"I already have a date," Chloe said. "Chris Rodriguez."

"Only if you win Queen," Chessie said, "*and* he doesn't have another date. If I win, then Chris is *my* date."

"What if Merlin wins?" Laurette said.

Three seconds of silence passed as the girls imagined this—then broke into peals of laughter.

"Yeah, right," P.J. said.

"Good one, Laurette," Lisi said.

"Okay, so Merlin probably won't be voted

King," Elle said. "That means he'll need a date to the dance. Any volunteers?"

Dead silence followed.

"P.J.?" Elle said. "What about you? You're a good sport."

"Not that good," P.J. said. "I'll go along with this, Elle, for your sake and the sake of the dance. But please, not Merlin. Anyone but Merlin."

"All right," Elle said. She checked her list of single boys for a good candidate. "How about Craig Jenkins?"

"Ewww," P.J. said. "Didn't he throw up in the pool? On Corned Beef and Cabbage Day?"

"That could happen to anybody," Elle said.

"He's one of Curt's best friends," Laurette said. "If we get him a date for the dance it will hit Curt where he lives."

"All right, you can fix me up with Craig," P.J. said. "I'll take one for the team. But my Homecoming is ruined!"

"I don't know, P.J.," Chessie said. "Can you really do better than Craig Jenkins? I'm not so sure."

"What about you?" P.J. said. "You have about as much chance of being Homecoming Queen as I do of winning Miss America. You'll be lucky to end up with Merlin."

"Hey, no fighting!" Elle said. "We're a team, remember? Thank you, P.J. You're showing true team spirit. Now, who's next. Lisi? Are you willing to go with Mike Mott?"

Elle got most of the cheerleaders to agree to a date with a boy who never had one before. These boys were mostly Curt's friends. Laurette was exempt, since her boyfriend, Darren, was planning to come home from college to take her to the dance.

Elle hoped the boys would go along with this . . . and why wouldn't they? Most of them had probably never dreamed they'd go to a dance with a cheerleader.

"This is the most important thing," Elle said. "What goes on in cheerleader HQ is just between us. Don't tell anyone about our secret plans. Remember your Cheerleader's Oath. Okay?"

"Okay," they said in unison; Elle watched their mouths to see whether anyone secretly wasn't saying it. But they all did.

"Guess what, Craig? I've got a surprise for you." Elle approached Craig Jenkins in the lunchroom. He had finished eating and was sitting alone doing a Sudoku puzzle.

"What is it? I don't like surprises," Craig said.

"This is a good surprise," Elle said. "I know someone who likes you."

Craig looked up from his book. His small, shaved head was perched on a skinny neck. He wore thick, heavy glasses and a T-shirt that said, MY OTHER T-SHIRT IS CLEAN.

It was too bad about the glasses, Elle thought. They were hiding very nice brown eyes.

"Is this some kind of joke?" Craig asked, looking around. "Am I about to get punked? Where's the camera?"

"You're not getting punked," Elle said. "I just thought you should know that P. J. Stoller wants to go to the Homecoming Dance with you."

"Haven't you heard?" Craig said. "There isn't going to be a Homecoming Dance."

"If Curt wins," Elle said.

"Well—" Craig went back to his book, as if to say, "Case closed."

"Well, what?" Elle said.

"Well, of course he's going to win," Craig said. "The latest poll has him up by twenty points. But don't feel bad. You're crushing Merlin. I don't think even he's voting for himself."

Elle tried to hide her annoyance. "Just in case

there is a dance," she said, "wouldn't you like to have a date for it? A date with an adorable, popular cheerleader?"

"How do you know she likes me?" Craig asked.

"She told me," Elle said.

Just then P.J. popped her head into the lunchroom. She smiled at Craig and gave him an enticing little wave.

"See?" Elle said. "I told you. Why don't you go out there right now and ask her to the dance?"

"I know this is some kind of trick," Craig said, but Elle could see that he was tempted.

"I swear, no trick," Elle said. "If there's a dance, P.J. will go with you." She pulled his chair away from the table and helped him to his feet. "Go on, now. She's waiting."

She pushed him toward the door. He walked, robotlike, out of the lunchroom. Elle kept her fingers crossed.

Don't blow it, P.J., she prayed silently.

A few minutes later, Craig returned, beaming. "Guess I'll have to dig out my other T-shirt," he said, tugging on the one he was wearing, to make sure she got the joke. "You know, the clean one."

P.J. peeked through the door and gave Elle the A-OK sign. So far, so good.

"Maybe you could even wear a non-T-shirt shirt," Elle said carefully. She didn't want to push things too far.

"What—you mean like a tank top?" he said.

"Or whatever."

On her way out of the lunchroom, Elle saw something fly into Maggie's hair: a piece of candy corn. Elle turned around to see where it had come from. Merlin was reloading his rubber band with another piece of candy.

Aha. Elle froze, waiting to see what would happen next. Neither Merlin nor Maggie were aware that she was watching.

Maggie picked the candy corn out of her hair and turned around. She saw Merlin with his rubber band, two tables away. She threw the piece of candy corn back at him. It landed in his plate of mashed potatoes.

She did it! Elle thought. Maggie threw the candy back.

This was big. This was exciting. This meant that Maggie liked Merlin. Of all people! Bibi had said it was a sure sign.

If Elle could get a date for Merlin, she could get a date for anyone. Everybody knew that. And to match him up with Curt's campaign manager—

what a coup that would be for her campaign!

Elle waited to see what happened next, but the bell rang. Lunch period was over. Maggie got up, bused her tray, and left the room. Elle scurried after her.

"Maggie, wait!" Elle called.

"If you're upset about the latest poll, I promise I use totally scientific methods," Maggie said. She handed Elle a questionnaire she'd been passing out to all the students. The first question on it read: *On election day I will vote for: a. A tubby tuba player who's never won anything in his life; b. An empty-headed blonde cheerleader; c. Curt Blaylock, the smartest boy in the school.*

"Hey," Elle protested. "That's totally not fair." No wonder her poll numbers were so low, she thought.

"File a complaint with Ms. Mikulski if you have a problem with it," Maggie said.

Elle crumpled up the paper and tossed it away. "That's not why I stopped you. I wanted to ask you something. Do you like Merlin Jones?"

Elle thought she saw a look of fear flicker across Maggie's face for a second. "I respect everyone in this school as a human being," Maggie said. She was being evasive.

"That's not what I mean. Do you *like* like him? You can tell me. I know he likes you."

"He does not," Maggie said. "And anyway, how could you know that?"

"I have my ways," Elle said.

"It's none of your business," Maggie said. "But since you asked, no, I do not like Merlin Jones. Of all people."

"Are you saying that if he asked you to the Homecoming Dance you would say no?" Elle said.

"Wake up, Elle. There isn't going to be a Homecoming Dance."

"Oh, yes, there is," Elle said. "And you're going. As Merlin's date."

"Get away from me!" Maggie said. "I do not like Merlin Jones. End of story." She marched defiantly away.

She's lying, Elle said to herself. Maggie liked Merlin. She just wasn't ready to admit it yet.

Chapter 10

"YOU MEAN you actually like him?" Elle asked Tamila. "For real?"

Tamila nodded. She had just confessed to having a crush on Matt Reiss. But Tamila was a freshman and afraid Matt didn't know she was alive.

Elle thought that that was impossible. Matt was kind of a schlumpy guy best known for being the student manager of the boys' basketball team. Tamila was adorable and a cheerleader, too.

"This is perfect," Elle said. "Ask him to the Homecoming Dance. If he says yes, that's another vote for us."

"I can't." Tamila fidgeted, twisting her sneakered toe on the floor. "What if he says no?"

"I bet he won't," Elle said. "But if you want, I'll ask him for you. I know him a little bit. I used to be his assistant."

"Assistant what?" Tamila asked.

"Assistant to the boys' basketball team manager," Elle said.

"You were?" Tamila said. Since she was a freshman, this was news to her. The year before, Elle had helped manage the boys' basketball team as a way of getting closer to Hunter. And it had worked.

"Long story," Elle said. "The point is, I'll talk to him."

"Awesome," Tamila said. "Thanks, Elle."

Elle found Matt in the hall during a morning break. "Do you have a date for Homecoming yet?" she asked.

"Homecoming? I thought that was canceled," Matt said. "The dance part, anyway."

"Over my dead body," Elle said. "All you have to do is vote for me, and the dance will happen."

"I could vote for you, but why bother? Curt's going to win anyway," Matt said.

"That's crazy talk!" Elle hated it when people said that to her. "Don't you believe in democracy? One student, one vote? This isn't Curt's personal kingdom, you know. If we don't like what he's doing, we can change things."

"Yeah, whatever," Matt said.

"So anyway, I know a girl who likes you, but she's too shy to ask you to the dance. Interested?"

"Who is it?"

"Tamila Vines. You're impressed now, right? A cheerleader, totally cute. Huh? Huh?"

Matt leaned forward, and Elle knew he was interested. "Yeah, sure she's cute," he said. "I might ask her out, now that I know she likes me."

"Excellent!" Elle's heart rose like the elevator at Saks—straight up to Finer Designers.

"But not to the dance," Matt said.

The elevator stalled at Housewares. "What? Why not?"

"There's a rumor going around—"

"What? What rumor?"

"I heard that I should be careful about getting fixed up for the dance," Matt said. "I heard you've got some kind of plot going where all the cheerleaders are going to ask geeky guys to the dance and then stand them up, just to be mean."

"What?!" Elle was horrified. "I'd never do something like that!"

"Other people are saying that even if the

cheerleaders show up for the dance, they're going to do something to embarrass their dates."

"That is so paranoid," Elle said. "I can't believe anybody would think that my cheerleaders would do something so mean."

"That's the word going around," Matt said, "from some pretty reliable sources."

"Who? Who's saying this?"

"I don't actually know who started it," Matt said. "But someone told me that someone told him that a cheerleader told him this herself."

"A cheerleader? Which one? You have to tell me!"

Matt shrugged. "Sorry. He didn't say."

"This is crazy. It's a total lie!"

"Maybe. But why take chances? I'm going to forget about the dance. That's what everyone else is doing. Craig Jenkins said he told P. J. Stoller to forget it—he's not going anywhere near the dance that night."

"So he dumped her?" Elle was outraged. "Over a silly rumor?"

"Well, he did ask her to come over to his house and play video games instead, but she told him no."

"I don't blame her," Elle said. "Video games are no substitute for a dance."

"It's too risky," Matt said. "I'm going to pass."

"But I don't want to hurt anyone," Elle said. "I'm trying to make people happy."

Matt shrugged. Then he schlumped away. Elle was stunned. She needed a pep talk, badly.

She flipped open her cell and called Hunter.

"It happened again," she said. She'd been keeping him up to date on her campaign.

"What?" Hunter said. "Your matchmaking plan isn't working?"

"Someone sabotaged it," Elle said.

"Curt?" Hunter asked.

"I don't know," Elle said. "But somehow, somebody from his side found out about my plan. They're spreading these horrible rumors that I'm setting up some kind of mean practical joke. They're saying that the cheerleaders want to embarrass their dates! Can you believe that?"

"It's brilliant," Hunter said, "but really mean."

"My plan never even had a chance to work," Elle said. "Who is doing this to me?"

"Maybe Laurette is right," Hunter said. "Maybe one of the cheerleaders is giving away your secrets."

"But that can't be," Elle insisted.

"Don't worry, Elle," Hunter said. "It's not over yet. You still have time to make your message heard."

In the background, Elle heard someone say, "Hunter, get over here. Your beaker's about to explode!"

"I better go," Hunter said. "I'm in chem lab and it looks like my experiment is going bad."

"You're not the only one," Elle said.

"Keep your chin up," Hunter said. "You've had problems before, and you always find an answer. You can do it again."

"Thanks." At least Hunter believed in her. That was something.

Elle clicked off and went to her locker, where she found another note: *Meet me at the Haunted House after school—Deep Ghost.*

Elle would be there. Maybe this time she'd get some answers.

Chapter 11

IT WAS almost Halloween, and the Haunted House was open for business. This time, Elle had to pay to get in. Luckily, school had just let out for the day, so only a few kids had arrived.

She walked in, blocking out the spooky music, the screams, the cackles, the flutter of bats' wings. Only one thing scared her now: the end of school dances, forever!

She stepped into a tunnel whose walls whirled and twirled, making her dizzy. "Deep Ghost?" she whispered. "Are you here?"

No answer. At the end of the tunnel was a door with a glow-in-the-dark handprint. PUSH HERE TO ENTER, a sign said in blood-red paint. Elle put her hand on the print, then quickly pulled it away.

"Ewww!" she shrieked, jumping back in horror. There was something slimy and gooey on the hand-print. "Disgusting!"

An evil laugh echoed through the tunnel. She pressed herself against the wall.

Okay, maybe other things still scared her a little bit, too.

Pull yourself together, she told herself. It was only a silly Halloween stunt. She rubbed her sticky hand on her jeans and kicked the door open with her foot.

She moved as quickly as she could past dummies dressed as witches and men hanging from nooses; disembodied heads; and a diorama showing a girl being sawed in half. Then, at last, a ghost jumped out from behind a cardboard tombstone.

"Boo!" the ghost shouted.

"There you are," Elle said. "Finally!"

"Boo!" the ghost said again.

"Stop kidding around," Elle said. "Just tell me what I need to know so I can get out of here."

The ghost stared quizzically at her through the holes in its sheet. "Boo," it said again, less forcefully this time.

"Deep Ghost?" Elle said.

"I don't know what you're talking about," the ghost finally said in a normal boy's voice. "Elle?" He pulled off his ghost costume.

"David?" It was David Reese, a boy in her homeroom—and an unlikely person to have inside information. "Sorry. I thought you were someone else."

"There are a few other ghosts as you get deeper into the house," David said. "Maybe you're looking for one of them?"

"Probably," Elle said. "I'm not sure exactly *who* I'm looking for."

"Well, it's not me." He pulled the sheet back on over his head. "Right through the torture chamber, past the giant spiderweb."

"Thanks," Elle said. She'd have to ask Deep Ghost to pick a less freaky meeting place next time.

"Elle, you made it," Deep Ghost said through the weird serial-killer-voice machine. He or she was perched at the top of a rickety staircase, rubber knife in hand and blood all over the sheet, as if ready to stab the next person who walked by.

"I guess you know about the terrible rumors going around," Elle said.

"Yes," the ghost said.

"Who's spreading them? Is it Curt and Maggie?"

Deep Ghost was quiet.

"What did you make me come here for if you won't tell me anything?" Elle asked in exasperation.

"I want to help you," Deep Ghost said. "But I can only say so much without getting myself into trouble. Yes, Curt and Maggie started those rumors."

"But how did they find out about my plan?" Elle asked.

"Somebody told them," Deep Ghost said.

"Who?"

"I can't say," Deep Ghost said. "But I can tell you this: follow the golden fingers."

"What? The golden fingers?"

"Yes. The trail of the golden fingers."

"What does that mean?"

Elle heard footsteps. Some kids were coming up behind her, laughing and joking.

"That's all I can say for now," Deep Ghost said. "Quick, get out of here. Someone's coming. And remember—follow the glow-in-the-dark footsteps."

"I thought you said follow the golden fingers."

"I did," the ghost said. "I meant, the glow-in-the-dark footsteps on the floor. Right in front of you. To find your way out of the Haunted House."

"Oh." Elle looked down and saw the glowing

footsteps on the floor. "Okay. But—"

"Go-o-o-o-o-o!" the ghost moaned. "Or I'll stab you with my rubber knife!"

"That wouldn't hurt too much," Elle said.

"Then I'll stain your white top with my fake blood! And nothing gets fake blood out. *Ooooooh!*"

"Okay, I'm going," Elle said.

She hurried out of the Haunted House, more confused than ever. Follow the golden fingers? What could that possibly mean?

Elle walked out of the gym and back through the school halls, which were empty now, and almost as spooky as the Haunted House. Her footsteps echoed on the floor. A door opened, and Elle jumped. It was only a teacher, headed home for the day, a pile of papers in her hand. Elle couldn't resist a glance at her fingers. Were they golden? No. More like ink-stained.

This Deep Ghost stuff is making me jumpy, Elle thought. *I've got to solve this mystery of the golden fingers soon, before I turn into a paranoid wreck.*

To calm down, Elle went home to work on Underdog's Halloween costume. He was going to be a cow-dog. She sewed up the costume, then made him try it on: a tiny red vest, a pair of little denim pants, a cowboy hat, and a handlebar mustache. He still needed something . . . a sheriff's badge, Elle decided.

"Underdog, you look adorable!" Elle said as he posed for her. He sneezed and blew his mustache off.

Elle stood up and paced in her room. Playing with Underdog usually soothed her, but not this time. The golden-fingers mystery nagged at her. She called Laurette.

"I've got to talk to you," she said.

"Come on over," Laurette said. "Mom's making blender drinks."

Chapter 12

"THAT MAKES *no sense*," Laurette said. She and Elle sat in her living room that evening before dinner. "Follow the golden fingers? Are you sure this Deep Ghost isn't leading you on somehow? Trying to distract you or send you down the wrong path?"

"Why would he do that?" Elle said.

"Is it a he?" Laurette said.

"I can't tell," Elle said. "Whoever it is, he or she uses one of those voice-changers to make their voice deep and scary. The machine sounds like a man, so I think of the ghost as a boy. But it could be anybody."

Laurette's mother, Margarita Smythe, walked in carrying a tray of foamy pink drinks. She was wearing a wasp-waisted red-and-white gingham dress with white socks and black Mary Janes. With her black hair styled in two knots over her ears, she could have been Minnie Mouse. Elle wanted to compliment her on her Halloween costume, but she was afraid to, because she wasn't sure it *was* for Halloween. Everything Margarita wore looked like a costume.

"What are these drinks?" Elle asked, taking a glass.

"Pink Squirrel smoothies," Margarita said. "Try one, they're yummy."

Elle tasted it. It had a cherry vanilla flavor. "Mmmm," she said, licking the pink mustache off her upper lip. Laurette's mom was always good for exotic treats and fun afternoons.

"Mom, if someone said to you, 'Follow the golden fingers,' what would you think?" Laurette asked.

"I'd think they were crazy," Margarita said.

"But what do you think it means?" Elle asked.

"I don't know," Margarita said. "A gold statue, maybe?"

"Maybe," Elle said. "Have you seen one lately?"

Margarita shook her head. "Don't look at me."

"Me, either," Laurette said. "Wait—what about

in the trophy case in the gym? There are lots of little gold statues in there."

"Let's look there tomorrow," Elle said. "Maybe there's some secret message hidden inside one of them or something."

"What about this?" Margarita scanned a bookshelf and pulled out a DVD from her movie collection. It was *Goldfinger*. The cover showed Sean Connery in a tux with a gun; a fat, balding blond guy; and a naked girl with golden skin. "It's an old James Bond movie," Margarita said.

"Maybe that's a clue," Laurette said.

"Let's watch it," Elle said.

Laurette popped it into the DVD player. Jazzy horns blasted behind Shirley Bassey's voice as she sang the theme song. *"Gold*fingah, . . . *the man with the Midas touch . . ."*

"Cool theme song," Elle said. "I kind of feel like it sums up my life right now."

They watched as the evil villain, Goldfinger (the fat guy), murdered people by smothering them in gold paint.

"What a weird way to murder people," Elle said.

"But simple," Laurette said.

"You don't think the ghost is warning me about murder, do you?" Elle said.

"I don't think so," Laurette said. "Not even Curt would kill to be president of our lame school."

When the movie was over, Elle said, "That was good, but I'm still not sure what it has to do with me."

"Let's try the trophy case tomorrow," Laurette said. "Maybe there's a secret in one of the gold statues."

"I really don't think you'll find anything in here," Ms. Blumly, the gym teacher, said the next day. She unlocked the trophy case in the gym lobby for Elle and Laurette. "But be my guest."

Most of the trophies were silver-colored, but there were a few gold ones. Elle picked up the biggest gold trophy—Boys' Varsity Baseball League Champions, 1974—and touched its tiny fingers. "Could there be a secret compartment in here or something?" she asked.

Ms. Blumly laughed. "I'd be awfully surprised."

Laurette checked all the statues, too. She and Elle looked under the bases, read the inscriptions over and over, even tried breaking off the statues' heads—but they found no interesting clues.

"I guess this was a stupid idea," Elle said. Just then, a group of ninth-grade girls came out of gym class. Amy Desoto's toes twinkled in her sandals.

Elle's eyes drifted up toward her hands. Amy was wearing gold nail polish.

"Oh, my God, that's it!" Elle cried. She ran up to Amy and nearly tackled her. "Golden fingers! Golden fingers!" she cried.

"Yeah, what about it?" Amy said.

"We need to have a talk," Laurette said.

"About what?" Amy said.

"About your nail polish," Elle said.

"I'm not talking to you about my nail polish," Amy said. "I hardly know you."

Elle looked at Laurette. Amy did seem like an unlikely source of betrayal. As she said herself, she hardly knew them. But the election was crucial. They could leave no stone unturned.

"Just show up at Petronio's Pizza today," Elle said, "for your interrogation."

"What? I'm not doing that," Amy said.

"You have to." Laurette flashed a tin sheriff's badge she'd bought that day for Underdog's cow-dog costume. "Department of Cowboy Justice."

"You made that up," Amy said.

"Did I?" Laurette said. "Take a chance and find out. Disobeying the department can lead to criminal prosecution by the school board of elections. But if you think you're above the law—"

"All right, whatever," Amy said. "I'll be there. Just stop talking like that."

When they saw Amy at Petronio's later that afternoon, her fingernails were no longer gold. They were pink.

"What happened to your fingernails?" Elle asked. "Weren't they gold before?"

"I took that nail polish off," Amy said. "It wasn't worth being tackled in the gym lobby over it."

"Why did you put on pink polish?"

"Because I borrowed some from my friend Kari, and that was the only color she had," Amy said.

"Why were you wearing gold polish before?" Elle asked.

"Um, it went with my skirt?" Amy said. "What's your problem?"

Elle glanced at Laurette. They weren't getting anywhere with Amy. Either she was a very clever liar or she was totally innocent. And Elle didn't think Amy was all that clever.

Laurette thrust her face in Amy's. "What do you know about sabotaging Elle's campaign?"

"What? Nothing," Amy said. "I swear. I have no idea what you're talking about. Have you guys gone psycho?"

"You know what, Elle?" Laurette said. "I believe her."

Elle sighed. "So do I." Amy just didn't seem like a spy. The gold nail polish was probably a coincidence.

"Can I go to my tanning appointment now?" Amy said.

"Go ahead," Elle said.

"Thank you, Sheriff. Good luck in Cow Town."

"I've got the results of the latest poll," Laurette told Elle, who was slouched against her locker, the next day.

"And—?" Elle sat up, excited.

"Reslouch," Laurette said. "You're not going to like it. You're thirty points behind Curt. You're even a couple of points behind Buzz, the Killer Bee." Buzz was the football team's mascot, a boy who wore a big bee suit and tried to dump water on the other mascots' heads. "But you're way ahead of Merlin. If that helps."

"It doesn't help," Elle said. "Number two isn't good enough. If I don't win it's the end of dances! We've got to find out who's been sabotaging us, and then make one last push before the election."

"I think the debate will be your best chance to

impress people," Laurette said.

"If anyone shows up," Elle said. "It's not exactly the most highly anticipated event of the season."

"Mikulski made it mandatory this year," Laurette said. "During assembly. So the whole school will be there, against their will."

"Captive audience. Great."

"They could be hostile," Laurette said. "You've got to get them on your side. We've got to prepare. We can't leave this to chance. The first debate is crucial."

"All right," Elle said. "We'll plan, but secretly. We can't have any more leaks."

"So, that means we can't tell anyone our plans," Laurette said. "Not even the cheerleaders."

"But we can trust them," Elle said. "They took—"

"I know, I know, they took the oath." Laurette rolled her eyes. "Some people break their promises, you know. It happens."

"Not a cheerleader," Elle said. "Not a real one."

"Well, just to be on the safe side, let's not tell them anything, and see what happens," Laurette said. "Okay?"

"Okay," Elle said. She didn't like it. But she knew Laurette was right. They couldn't take any chances.

Chapter 13

From: hperry
To: elliebelly
Re: big debate tomorrow
Date: Thurs 4 Oct 8:34 PM

how u doing, girlie? got your speech all ready? watch out for curt—he's a good debater.

wishing you luck . . .

hunter

From: elliebelly
To: hperry
Re: big debate tomorrow

I'm freaking out!!!! My speech is not ready. I have no idea what to say! How can I ever beat Curt? What made me think I could do this? it's going to be a disaster!!!!!

Miss miss miss you . . .

Elle

From: hperry
To: elliebelly
Re: big debate tomorrow
Date: Thurs 4 Oct 9:21 PM

calm down. you'll be fine. i've seen you give big rousing speeches that win people over. you're GREAT at it. and totally charming. stop worrying! you can send me your speech after you write it, if you want, and I'll read it over. but i know it will rock!!!

hunter

From: elliebelly
To: hperry
Re: big debate tomorrow
Date: Thurs 4 Oct 9:30 PM

Okay, but what should I say? I don't even know where to start.

From: hperry
To: elliebelly
Re: big debate tomorrow
Date: Thurs 4 Oct 10:04 PM

well, curt will probably try to show he's the most serious, smartest, experienced candidate. so you can either say "i'm smart and serious too," or find something else to say about yourself. something just as good as smart and serious, or even better. like "adorable!"

good luck.
hunter

I'm so lucky, Elle thought as she read Hunter's e-mails. He always supported her. He was the best boyfriend ever.

Everybody should have someone like Hunter in their lives, she thought. Who didn't need love and romance? There wasn't enough of it at Beverly. So Elle started writing. She wrote a speech about how the school needed more romance. But when she read it over, it seemed so . . . lightweight. Curt was probably expecting a speech like that from her. He'd be prepared with some kind of rebuttal. So she wrote another speech. A serious speech. Listing her experience, her credentials, her leadership ability.

That ought to work, she thought as she read it over. *I'll show them that I can be as serious as anyone.*

"Let me check you out." Laurette scanned Elle's outfit: a navy blue skirt suit with a white blouse and a red scarf. "Red, white, and blue—it's hokey, but it works," Laurette said.

Elle and Laurette were at cheerleader HQ for a last-minute briefing before the debate. As Laurette had recommended, no one else was present, in spite of Elle's objections that the cheerleaders were trustworthy.

"Okay, you've got your index cards?" Laurette asked.

Elle nodded. She'd copied her speech onto index cards so that it would be easy to keep track of her points and responses.

"You practiced your opening statement and closing words?" Laurette asked.

"Over and over again," Elle said.

"I guess you're ready, then," Laurette said with an encouraging smile. "Let's go."

★ ★ ★

"And I say to you," Curt proclaimed as he stood at the podium and lectured the student audience an hour later. "I say to you, students of Beverly Hills High, that my opponents, Elle Woods and Merlin Jones, don't have what it takes to be your president. And today I will demonstrate that. What you have before you—" He swept his arm out toward the stage to indicate the chairs where Elle and Merlin were sitting. "—Are a marching-band musician and a rah-rah cheerleader. Neither one has political experience or leadership qualities. Neither one is the smartest student at BHH. Only I am. I am the only candidate with *gravitas*."

Tepid applause followed. Curt had gone the serious route, just as Elle expected. She watched as the kids text-messaged each other, checked their messages, and shot spitballs at unsuspecting victims. *If Merlin and Maggie were out there, they'd be throwing candy at each other,* Elle thought. But Merlin was sitting on the stage next to her, and Maggie was backstage, clipboard in hand, anxiously watching Curt speak.

"Only I have an IQ of 141, straight A's in every subject, and a year's worth of experience as your leader. I began the Full Disclosure Rule, stating that every student must turn in cheaters or be punished themselves. And I proposed the new dress-code legislation, requiring every student to wear full business attire, including ties for the boys, to school every day. This proposal didn't pass, but with luck, this year it will."

There was dead silence.

I can't believe anybody would vote for this guy, Elle thought. Nobody wanted to wear business clothes to school. But the students obviously had no idea what Curt's ideas were. They weren't listening to a word he said.

"And now I graciously cede the floor to my opponents," Curt said.

"Thank you, Curt." Ms. Mikulski, who was moderating, clapped heartily. "We'll see you again for the rebuttal. Merlin?"

Merlin picked up his tuba and went to the podium. "Curt is right. I am a tuba player in the marching band. Is there anything wrong with that?"

He waited for a response from the crowd, but none came.

"I said, let's hear it for the marching band!"

In the audience, a couple students coughed, but there was no cheering.

Merlin went on with his presentation. "Instead

of giving you a boring speech, I thought I'd serenade you with my tuba." He put the tuba to his lips, then stopped to add, "By the way, if you vote for me, you'll get to hear a tuba serenade every morning at assembly. It's an added bonus: two for one—me and my tuba. This song is the theme from *Battlestar Galactica*."

Bwat, bwat, bwat bwat bwat . . . As Merlin huffed and puffed on his tuba, the students grew even more restless.

I've got to do something to get their attention, Elle thought. She could try her hardest to show them she was superserious, but what good would it do if they didn't notice?

Merlin finished his tuba solo. "Just try and rebut that," he said. He returned to his seat.

"Elle?" Ms. Mikulski said.

"Thank you, Ms. Mikulski," Elle said. "With all due respect to Mr. Blaylock, I challenge him when he says he has more gravity than I do."

"Gravitas," Laurette whispered from backstage. "He said *gravitas.*"

Whatever. It was too late to change it now, and besides, very few people seemed to have noticed.

"I may be a cheerleader, but that is only part of who I am," Elle said. "I'm also a good student, and

I care about this school. I helped manage the championship basketball team last year. Over the summer I learned to surf and won a bikini-design contest." There were a few snickers from the audience. "I helped stop a greedy developer from illegally building on a protected beach. That wasn't easy. And it was very, very serious."

The audience was still distracted. What could she do to get them to wake up and pay attention?

"Life-or-death serious," she added. "I would also like to remind Curt that I'm not just a cheerleader—I'm captain of the squad. That is a leadership position. And if you think it's easy to control a squad of cheerleaders, you're crazy."

"Do a backflip!" someone shouted. Elle ignored him.

"In conclusion, I am a very serious person with a strong background in politics and leadership. Thank you."

Scattered applause accompanied her as she sat down.

"Okay. Rebuttals," Ms. Mikulski said. "Curt?"

Curt went to the podium. "Elle, what is the square root of pi?"

Elle was surprised by the question. "What does that have to do with anything?"

"Just answer the question."

"I don't know," Elle said.

"Merlin?"

Honk. Merlin tooted on his tuba in response.

"It's 1.77245385," Curt said. "My fellow Bees, can we afford to have a leader who doesn't know such basic math questions as this? I ask you as your peer, your comrade, but mostly, as your superior."

"Who cares?" somebody shouted from the auditorium.

"We'll have time for questions later," Ms. Mikulski said. "Are you finished, Curt?"

"Just one more thing," Curt said. "I don't think many of you will vote for someone who plays the tuba instead of talking. But you might be seduced by a pretty smile, nice clothes, and golden-blonde hair. If you are—think very carefully. Think twice. Think three times, if your brains can stand the strain. Because pretty blonde hair doesn't help you make decisions, or take a stand, or forge new paths to the future of this school. Thank you."

Elle glanced at Laurette, who frowned. So much for being serious. In that department, she'd never be able to beat Curt. She didn't even want to.

Chapter 14

"WE DEFINITELY need a new tactic," Laurette said after the debate. She and Elle sat under a tree in the courtyard doing postgame analysis. They agreed that things hadn't gone in their favor.

"The trouble is," Laurette added, "we've been through so many plans already."

"Some of those plans were good," Elle said. "They would have worked if Curt hadn't found out about them."

"You mean if someone hadn't told him," Laurette said. Chessie sauntered toward them. "*Shhh*. Here comes one of our top suspects now."

"Elle, you were *so great* in the debate this afternoon," Chessie said. "It showed real courage, taking on Curt at his own game. 'Gravity.' That was hilarious."

"But no one takes me seriously yet," Elle said.

"What do you expect?" Chessie said. "You don't have to be a genius to figure out that Curt's going to win the election. But that's not the point, is it?"

"Actually, it is," Laurette said.

Chessie reached up to scratch her nose. That was when Elle noticed it. Gold nail polish on her fingernails. *Goldfinger.* She gave Laurette a secret pinch.

"You're not actually expecting to beat him, are you?" Chessie said.

"Why else would I run?" Elle said.

"For the attention!" Chessie said. "After this election, everyone in school will know who you are. It's a brilliant bid for popularity."

"But I'm not running to get attention," Elle said. "Or popularity. I'm campaigning so I can be school president, and stop Curt from canceling all the dances."

Maggie passed through on the other side of the courtyard. Chessie ran after her like a puppy. "Maggie! I've got to ask you something!"

"Did you see that?" Laurette said when Chessie was gone.

Elle nodded. "I saw it."

"Gold fingernail polish," Laurette said. "That's a pretty big clue."

"But she's a cheerleader," Elle said. "Why would she betray me?"

"She's got plenty of reasons," Laurette said. "She's always been jealous of you. She wishes she were captain instead of you. And she's running for Homecoming Queen. Maybe she made a deal with Curt and Maggie. Maybe they're helping her somehow." She rubbed her chin. "I've got it! They could fix the Homecoming Queen election in exchange for her bringing them damaging evidence about you."

"That's crazy," Elle said. "If she's Homecoming Queen, she's going to want there to be a dance. Otherwise, what's the point? And anyway, Chloe is running for Queen, too. Why would Chessie be the one who's going over to the dark side? Why not Chloe?"

"Because Chessie is the one with gold fingernails," Laurette said. "Just like the ghost said."

"I just don't see Chessie selling me out," Elle said.

"Why not?" Laurette said. "I smell a rat—a golden rat."

"We'll test her," Elle said. "Then you'll see."

"That's right," Laurette said. "You'll see that

Chessie's been the leak all along."

"No, you'll see that she's *not* the leak," Elle said.

"Bet you a Pink Squirrel she is," Laurette said, holding out her pinky.

Elle linked pinkies with her. "It's a bet."

Chapter 15

"WELCOME TO the annual Homecoming Pageant," Mr. Wrightsman said.

Mr. Wrightsman, the assistant principal, was wearing a tuxedo for the occasion and had his dark hair slicked back more than usual. As assistant principal, he seemed to be more a figurehead. While Ms. Mikulski, the principal, did all the real work, Mr. Wrightsman hosted talent shows, parents' teas, and other social events.

He grinned, his perfect teeth sparkling in the stage lights.

The Homecoming Pageant was held on a flower-festooned stage in the middle of the football field at halftime the Saturday before Homecoming.

"You all know me; I don't need any introduction with this crowd." He paused for laughter that never came. Half the football fans were off getting snacks.

"This is your chance to see your King and Queen nominees in action before you vote for them next Friday," Mr. Wrightsman said. "So let's welcome them now!"

The marching band, minus Merlin, played while five girls and two boys marched onto the stage. The girls wore matching long white gowns and the boys—Chris and Merlin—wore tuxedos. Elle and Laurette pushed through the crowd in the stands to get a better look.

"Hey," Elle said. "Nice nail polish."

The girls all sported fresh manicures with identical nail polish—in gold.

"They're all Goldfingers!" Laurette said.

"That's why Chessie was wearing gold polish," Elle said. "She had to, for the pageant."

"That doesn't mean she's not Goldfinger," Laurette said.

"It doesn't mean she is, either," Elle said. "You're going to owe me a Pink Squirrel."

"Here they are . . ." Mr. Wrightsman sang, to the tune of the Miss America song, *"the Homecoming nominees . . ."*

"God, he's such a dweeb," Laurette said.

"We'll conduct short interviews with each nominee," Mr. Wrightsman said. "And then they'll have a chance to show us a talent. Let's start with the guys. Fellas, step over here."

Chris and Merlin stepped up to the microphone. "Now, Chris," Mr. Wrightsman said. "Why do you want to be Beverly Hills High Homecoming King?"

Chris shrugged. "I don't know. I thought it might be cool."

"No other reason?"

"No. It seemed easy. All my friends said I'd probably win. I like to do easy stuff."

"Well put!" Mr. Wrightsman said. "Words of wisdom: 'I like to do easy stuff.' Okay. Merlin, what about you? What made you decide to run against a handsome, popular guy like Chris?"

Merlin reached for his tuba, which was sitting on the edge of the stage, ready for his talent act. But Mr. Wrightsman stopped his hand.

"Oh, no. You can't get away with talking through your tuba this time. Use words."

"Well, I always run for everything," Merlin said. "Everybody knows that."

"He always runs for everything!" Mr. Wrightsman

bleated. "Charming, charming. Anything else?"

Merlin glanced at Maggie. Elle caught the look.

"There's somebody I want to impress," he said, eyes on Maggie. He even gave her a little wave. Elle turned to see what Maggie's reaction was, but Maggie turned away as if she hadn't seen anything.

"Wanting to impress people," Mr. Wrightsman said. "Always a good reason to do anything. Okay, thank you, gentlemen. We'll get back to you. Merlin and Chris, everybody! Please do a little walk and turn for the audience."

Chris walked around Mr. Wrightsman, spun around on his heel like a backup singer for James Brown, and retired to the back of the stage, where he lounged casually. Merlin waddled around in a circle like a lost duck.

"On to the ladies," Mr. Wrightsman said. "A lovely crop this year. First up, in alphabetical order—we wouldn't want to play favorites—we have Chloe Gaitskill."

Chloe walked over to Mr. Wrightsman while the crowd clapped and whistled. "Chloe, if you become Homecoming Queen, what will you try to accomplish?"

"If elected Homecoming Queen, I promise to use the office to struggle for world peace, to help children everywhere, and to erase hunger from our planet."

"Ambitious, very ambitious, Chloe," Mr. Wrightsman said. "We like to see that. Good luck. Okay, give us the walk and the spin, and . . . Anna Goodrow?"

Chloe walked and did her spin as Anna went up to the mike.

"I'm a realist, Mr. Wrightsman," Anna said. "As Homecoming Queen, I know I don't have the power to solve a lot of the world's problems, or even those right here in Beverly Hills. So my only goal, as Queen, is to look good. Chris and I are both good-looking. If he wins, we'll look good together, all year long."

"Deep, very deep," Mr. Wrightsman said. He touched his heart. "Gets you right here, doesn't it?"

Kyra Holmbeck said she wanted to see her picture in the school newspaper. Jessica McMartin said her mother had been a Homecoming Queen and told her if she won she could have a new car.

And then it was Chessie's turn.

"Francesca," Mr. Wrightsman said, using Chessie's real name. "Why do you want to be Homecoming Queen?"

Chessie took a deep breath. She kept her eyes on Chris the whole time she spoke. Elle knew he was the real reason she wanted to be Homecoming Queen so badly.

"Well, I wanted to be captain of the cheerleaders," Chessie said. "But I'm such a good cheerleader the other members of the team didn't want me wasting my energy on administrative stuff. That's what they told me, anyway."

Laurette elbowed Elle. "See? See?"

"And I thought about running for president, but everybody knows Curt's unbeatable, so why make a fool of myself? Elle's taking care of that for us, which is so brave and nice of her."

"Hmmm . . ." Elle said.

"Everybody always says the Homecoming Queen is the epitome of beauty and popularity and grace, and I like it when people say that about me—as often as possible. So here I am." Chessie smiled, did an awkward spin, tripped over her own toes and nearly landed on her butt. Mr. Wrightsman propped her up and saved her at the last minute.

"There you have it," Mr. Wrightsman said. "Noble motives, one and all. Remember these words when you go to the polls next Friday. And now, the talent. Chris, what will you be doing for us today?"

"I'll be passing a lacrosse ball back and forth with my buddy Brent," Chris said.

"Fascinating," Mr. Wrightsman said.

"How much more of this do we have to sit through?" Laurette asked.

Elle looked at the scoreboard clock, counting down the minutes until halftime was over. "Only about another half an hour," she said.

"I'm going for a soda," Laurette said. "I can't sit through another tuba solo by Merlin. Want anything?"

"Diet Coke," Elle said. "Thanks."

Elle watched the pageant carefully while Laurette was gone. Jessica and Kyra both sang the same Kelly Clarkson song, badly, while Anna did an Irish step dance and Chloe did a magic act. Chessie showed off her cheerleading skills, nearly decapitating Mr. Wrightsman with one of her kicks.

"Did I miss anything?" Laurette asked when she came back.

Elle hesitated. She wasn't sure how to answer.

"Let me put it this way," Laurette said. "Did I miss anything that I would have liked to have seen?"

That, knowing Laurette, Elle *could* answer. "No. No, you didn't."

"Did Chessie say anything else about how badly she wishes she could be president and captain instead of you?" Laurette asked.

"No," Elle said. "Because she doesn't."

"We'll see," Laurette said.

"Cheerleader's Oath," Elle said.

"Don't give me that," Laurette said. "The Cheerleader's Oath is grab all the attention you can, and trample anybody who gets in your way."

"You don't understand cheerleaders at all," Elle said. "That's why you're not one."

"No, I do understand them," Laurette said. "*That's* why I'm not one."

"I thought it was because you don't like the uniform," Elle said.

"There's that, too," Laurette said.

Chapter 16

"YOU SHOULD be the Homecoming Queen," Hunter said. Elle was on the phone with him, filling him in on the latest news. She was tired of phone calls and e-mails—she couldn't wait to see him in person again. But they were both so busy there was no time.

"You're the prettiest girl in the whole place," Hunter said. "And the most queenly."

"I've got too much to do already," Elle said. "Besides, I don't want to be Chris's date at the dance. All I care about is being with you."

"Me, too," Hunter said. "You can always be Homecoming Queen next year. In addition to cheer captain and school president. That will make one impressive resume."

"I'm not so sure about the president part," Elle said. "It's not looking good."

"You've got one more debate to go," Hunter said. "It doesn't matter who people want to vote for now. What matters is who they'll vote for on *election day*. A lot can happen between now and then."

"You're right," Elle said. "A lot can happen."

"You know the best way to get people to talk?" Bibi said as she gave Elle her weekly manicure. "Sit them in my chair. Or any salon chair. Especially if you wash their hair first, to get them nice and relaxed. Toss out one innocent icebreaker, and then stand back and listen to them blab."

"Really?" Elle said.

"Oh, yeah," Bibi said. "Lots of times they tell me more than I want to know. Like this one woman, a classic Beverly Hills wife and mother, married to a big producer; I won't name names . . . All I did was compliment her bag, and she starts telling me she's got a bag problem."

"What do you mean?" Elle asked.

"She can't stop buying bags. Those superexpensive ones, especially. You know, the ones that cost thousands of dollars?"

"But she can afford them, right?" Elle said. "If she's married to a big producer . . ."

"That's what I said," Bibi said. "Then she starts telling me how cheap her husband is. He reuses aluminum foil. Like, if he buys a grilled-cheese sandwich and it comes wrapped in foil, he saves it and reuses it until it's in tatters."

"Weird," Elle said.

"Yeah," Bibi said. "So his wife's bag obsession drives him nuts. He threatened to leave her if she didn't stop buying them."

"So, did she stop?"

"No," Bibi said. "She couldn't stop. She was addicted."

"Wow," Elle said. "What a terrible story. Did they get divorced?"

"Almost," Bibi said. "They're trying to work it out. They're both in twelve-step programs now. She's in Shoppers Anonymous, and he's in Cheapos Anonymous."

"I didn't know there was a Cheapos Anonymous," Elle said.

"Neither did I," Bibi said. "Till I heard this story. She sat right there in that very chair and spilled it all, week after week. They all do. Fill a room with nail-polish fumes and tongues start wagging."

"Hmmm," Elle said. "So that's how you get me to talk so much."

"I never use my power as a force for evil, Elle," Bibi said, "only for good."

"If only *I* had that power," Elle said. "I wish Deep Ghost would get in touch with me again. I need more clues."

"Send that ghost here," Bibi said. "I'll make her talk. If it's a girl."

"I would if I could," Elle said. "But I don't even know if it *is* a girl."

Elle got her wish on Monday morning: another note from Deep Ghost.

Lunchtime, the usual place, the note said.

It was the week of the election. Election day was that Friday. The last debate was scheduled for Thursday. Laurette's polls still showed Curt way ahead. Time was running out. Elle had only a few days to turn things around.

"You're totally screwing everything up," Deep Ghost said in the special ghost voice. "You're on the wrong track."

"So what's the right track?" Elle asked. "Why can't you just tell me what's going on?"

"Don't ever ask me that again," Deep Ghost said, "or I'll leave and never help you anymore."

"Okay, sorry," Elle said. "I just don't see why you have to be so vague: that's all."

"I have my reasons," Deep Ghost said.

"I'm sure you do," Elle said.

"Listen," Deep Ghost said, "you're going to lose the election—unless you find the link between Merlin and Curt."

"What do you mean, the link between them?" Elle asked.

"They have something in common," Deep Ghost said. "Find it, and you can use it against Curt and win the election."

"Look—just tell me." Elle was getting tired of the silly ghost stuff. "What is it?"

There were footsteps and voices in the Haunted House. Deep Ghost got spooked.

"Figure it out for yourself," the ghost said. "Gotta go. Bye!"

The footsteps got louder as they drew closer. Deep Ghost hurried away.

Elle wandered back through the Haunted House the way she had come in. She walked toward the footsteps. Suddenly, they stopped. Somebody said, "Shhh!"

Elle froze. She listened, but heard nothing else. She walked on.

She passed a row of upright cardboard coffins. A mummy popped out of one of them. The rest were closed, but two of them had feet.

Feet?

Feet, sticking out of the bottom. One pair of highly polished boys' size-eleven extra-wide black band shoes, and one pair of girls' size-six extra-narrow penny loafers, with dimes where the pennies should go.

Merlin. And Maggie.

What were they doing there? And why were they together?

Elle knew Merlin had a crush on Maggie. And she knew that Maggie liked him, too.

Was that what this was about? Or was it something more sinister?

Elle pretended to walk past the row of coffins and leave the Haunted House. Then she stopped, took off her shoes, and doubled back on tiptoe.

She stopped at the coffins. The feet were still there, facing each other. Elle heard a muffled, familiar sound—a smooching sound.

Kissing noises.

She couldn't believe it. Merlin and Maggie had sneaked into the Haunted House to kiss!

Elle wasn't sure what she should do with this

information. Should she shout, "Aha!" and let them know she'd caught them? Or should she keep it to herself for a while until she knew how to use the information best? What would Laurette have done?

Don't show your hand. Don't let them know they're caught until the time is right.

Elle sneaked out of the house and hurried off to find Laurette and tell her the news. She didn't know what it meant. But it had to mean something.

Chapter 17

"MERLIN AND Maggie?" Laurette said. "Kissing? I don't believe it."

"I saw it with my own eyes," Elle said. "Well, sort of. I saw their shoes."

"So, how can you be sure it was them?"

"Who else wears superwide band shoes and supernarrow penny loafers with dimes in them?" Elle said.

"True," Laurette said, "but things have been so weird lately. What if someone is framing them? Trying to make you *think* Maggie and Merlin were kissing?"

"Why would they do that?" Elle asked.

"I don't know," Laurette said. "Why does anybody

do anything? Your ghost friend seems pretty fishy. Maybe he's setting you up."

"I think it's for real," Elle said. "I've seen the looks they give each other. And they've been hurling candy at each other like there's no tomorrow."

"Hurling candy?"

"Bibi says if a boy throws candy at a girl, it's a sure sign he likes her. And vice versa."

"And what would she know about it?" Laurette said. "She's a manicurist."

"*And* a hairdresser," Elle said. "She knows a lot about life. She's very wise."

They were headed for the girls' locker room to pick up a yellow scarf Laurette had left there.

"I can't believe I left the gym without it," she said, in a mock Valley-girl voice. "My outfit is totally meaningless without that scarf. I've been walking around looking like a doofus all day."

"Please, Laurette, you know you look fine," Elle said, surveying Laurette's outfit.

Laurette wore a vintage circle skirt with white socks, saddle shoes, a black scoop-neck tee, and a red sweater. "I like it with the scarf, too, though."

"No, no, no, it's all wrong," Laurette said, continuing her Valley-girl impression. "Without the scarf it has no zip, no pizzazz. The scarf pulls it all together and says, 'nineteen-fifties French girl who's really into philosophy and cinema.' But subtly. A beret would be overkill."

"Let's get the scarf and get out of here."

They pushed open the locker-room doors. School was over for the day, but there were voices coming from one row of lockers. This was a little strange, since all the girls' after–school sports teams were already out on the fields, practicing.

All those meetings with Deep Ghost had made Elle careful and a little suspicious. She froze and put her finger to her lips. Laurette understood and fell silent.

"I don't see what you're so worried about, Maggie." It was a loud whisper. It was Chessie's voice.

Elle raised her eyebrows in surprise, and Laurette nodded as if she'd known it all along.

Of course. Chessie and Maggie.

"Curt's going to win the election for sure," Chessie said. "Elle can't beat him. She's no threat to you. And neither am I."

"We can't take any chances," Maggie said. "That's why I need you to swear to secrecy—again. You're a cheerleader, and you see Elle all the time. If she finds out what we're up to, the first person

I'll blame is you. And then . . ." There was an ominous pause. "You'll face the consequences."

"Not the Homecoming vote," Chessie said, panic in her voice. "I really, really want to be Homecoming Queen. I'll do anything . . . almost anything . . ."

"I know you will," Maggie said. "That's why you'll keep your mouth shut. Or I'll sabotage you the same as Elle. You'll never be Homecoming Queen. You won't even be in her court. You'll be the laughingstock of the school."

"Please don't do that, Maggie," Chessie said.

"Okay. Then you'll play along?"

"Yes. I promise," Chessie said.

"Good. When Curt wins, you can be in his cabinet. Secretary of Homecoming, or something like that. Okay?"

"Okay."

Elle heard feet shuffling, and she darted into the bathroom, where she and Laurette hid in a shower stall. They heard Chessie and Maggie leave, but stayed perfectly still a few minutes longer to make sure the coast was clear.

"I don't believe it," Elle said. "What is Chessie doing?"

"Sabotaging you, obviously," Laurette said. "Working with that horrible pinch-face Maggie. I

144

hate to say I told you so, Elle, but the Cheerleader's Oath is not the most binding legal document in the world. Chessie is doing you wrong."

"I still don't believe it," Elle said. "She wouldn't."

"Why not? I keep telling you, she's totally jealous of you. And she said herself she'd do anything to be Homecoming Queen—fat chance . . . Of course, with Pinch-face helping her cheat it *might* be possible. . . ."

"This still isn't proof," Elle said.

"It isn't?" Laurette said. "A clandestine meeting in the girls' locker room? Whispering about keeping her mouth shut? What more proof do you want?"

"What people say and what they do are two different things, sometimes," Elle said. "I want physical, concrete proof. I want to catch her red-handed."

"Forget about that," Laurette said. "You've got a big advantage now. We can use this information against Curt. We can use it to beat him. If we can expose his campaign manager as a cheat who's rigging the election for president *and* Homecoming, no one will vote for him. It's a corrupt regime. Then you'll win—and we'll do the twist together at your victory-slash-Homecoming Dance."

Elle sat down and leaned against the cold tiled wall. She had to give the matter some thought.

"If we expose Maggie it will hurt Chessie," she said. "She won't have a chance to be Queen. And it means so much to her."

"So?" Laurette said. "She doesn't deserve it. She's hurting you without giving it a thought."

"I just can't accept that," Elle said. "And that's not how I want to win. I want everyone to vote for me because they think I'll be a good president, not because Maggie's plotting and scheming behind the scenes."

"But don't you see?" Laurette said. "People *would* vote for you because they think you'd be good—except that Maggie keeps undermining your message. The voters have the wrong idea about you because of Maggie and Chessie's cheating. They took away any chance you ever had of winning fair and square. Now you have no choice but to expose them. It's the right thing to do. It's for the voters' own good. You've worked hard. You'd be a great school president. And Curt has cheated—or at least his campaign manager has. You deserve to win, Elle."

"I'll think about it," Elle said. "Maybe there's a way to show my strengths in the next debate."

"This is the perfect way," Laurette said. Elle could tell Laurette was getting a little frustrated.

But she needed some time to mull things over.

"I just don't want to hurt anyone," Elle said, "or jump to conclusions. If Chessie got hurt because of something I did, I'd feel terrible. What if she's innocent?"

"As your campaign manager, I'm telling you, you don't have to worry about that."

But Elle worried about it anyway.

Chapter 18

"PLEASE, ELLE, please," Laurette said. "Let me expose Chessie and Maggie as the two-faced liars they are. If you don't want to do it, I will."

Elle and Laurette were meeting in cheerleader HQ for a powwow, alone. Elle still hadn't decided what to do. But she was leaning away from Laurette's plan.

"You just don't want to give me that Pink Squirrel, do you," Laurette said. "Is that it?"

"Of course not," Elle said.

Elle began to notice a funny odor. She sniffed and made a face. "Do you smell that?" she asked. It was a toxic, fumy smell.

Laurette sniffed and nodded. "That's weird. I

wonder where's it coming from."

They sniffed around the room until they found the spot where the smell was strongest—right next to an air vent.

"It's coming through here," Laurette said. "What's on the other side of this vent?"

"I don't know," Elle said. "Let's go see."

They walked into the hall and to the room next door. The door was closed, but painted on it were the words *Band Equipment Room*.

"The vent must lead from here," Laurette said. She tried the door. It opened, but somebody pushed it shut and locked it before she could open it all the way.

"Hey!" she cried.

Elle knocked on the door. "Open up, whoever you are! We know you're in there!"

Silence.

"This is ridiculous," Laurette said. "Don't pretend you're not in there. We'll go get the janitor and make him unlock the door if you don't open it right now."

There was a crashing noise, and a groan. Elle banged on the door again. "Are you all right?"

The doorknob turned and clicked.

"It's unlocked now," Laurette said. She turned

the knob. The room was dark and smelled strongly of paint.

Elle switched on the light.

There stood Merlin. A can of gold spray paint lay on the floor, and his tuba sat on a sheet of newspaper. A pile of music stands lay tangled in a corner. He must have knocked them over in the dark.

"So that's what the smell was," Elle said. "Spray paint. We could smell it next door. Through the vent."

Merlin shrugged sheepishly. "I was just touching up my tuba. I like to keep it shiny. The gold rubs off if you play it all the time like I do."

Elle glanced at his fingers. They had splotches of gold paint on them.

"Goldfinger!" she cried. "It's you!"

"Goldfinger?" Merlin said. "What are you talking about?"

Elle went to the vent and peered through it. Nothing could be seen. But if smells could get through, maybe sounds could, too.

"Laurette, go to HQ and talk to yourself for a minute," Elle said.

"Talk to myself?"

"Just say anything, in a normal voice, the way you and I would talk to each other in there."

"Okay." Laurette disappeared, and a few seconds later Elle heard her say, "Merlin is a big, fat cheater."

Elle looked at Merlin. "Did you hear that?"

He tried to look innocent. "Hear what?"

"You heard it," Elle said. "I'm sorry it wasn't very nice. But what you've been doing isn't very nice, either."

"I haven't been doing anything!" Merlin insisted. "I told you, I just came in to spruce up my tuba."

"But you've spent a lot of time in here listening, haven't you?" Elle said. "Like, whenever we hold a campaign meeting? And discuss our plans?"

"No, no, really—"

Laurette returned. "Could you hear me?"

"Loud and clear," Elle said. "Okay, Merlin, why did you do it? Do you want to be school president so badly you'd cheat?"

"I *would* like to win something someday," Merlin said. "But I could never beat Curt. Coming in second would be nice for a change, though, instead of last."

"So you sabotaged our campaign just so you could come in second?" Laurette said. "That's crazy."

"There had to be another reason," Elle said. "Spill it!"

"No, really, nothing," Merlin said.

"He's protecting somebody," Laurette said.

"And I think I know who," Elle said. "Merlin, tell me the truth or I'll go to Maggie and tell her we caught you spying on us. I'll tell her how clumsy you were to get caught so easily. I wonder if that will make her mad."

She waited as Merlin's eyes darted nervously from her to Laurette.

"Okay, I'll tell you," he finally said. "It will all come out soon anyway."

"Can we go next door?" Laurette said. "The paint fumes are really strong in here."

They sat down in HQ and listened as Merlin poured out his story.

"I was doing it for Maggie," he said. "I'm in love with her."

"Ewww—really?" Laurette said.

Elle slapped her lightly on the hand. "Laurette— the heart wants what it wants."

"I guess."

"She can be attractive," Elle said.

"She's too pinchy-faced," Laurette said. "It's a personality thing."

"She's beautiful," Merlin said. And in spite of all he'd done to Elle, his sentiment warmed her heart.

"She's superambitious," Merlin said. "Also, she hates school dances, just like Curt. I guess she never had a date to one before, either."

"So she got you to spy on us by listening through the vent?" Elle said.

"Yes," Merlin said. "She was afraid you would beat Curt in the election, so she thought we should sabotage your campaign. She tried to get one of your cheerleaders to talk, but they all refused."

Elle smiled at Laurette in triumph. "See, I told you."

"But what about Chessie?" Laurette said. "We heard her scheming with Maggie just yesterday."

"I don't know," Merlin said. "Maybe she caved in to the pressure later. All I know is, my sweet Magillicutty needed my help."

"Your sweet Magillicutty?" Elle said.

"Ick," Laurette said. "Please, spare us the grosser details."

"No, tell us everything," Elle said.

"I heard all your plans, to make cookies, to play the underdog," Merlin said. "I heard you practicing your serious speech."

"You rat!" Elle cried. "Every time we made progress, you did something to set us back. What you did was really mean, Merlin, and really bad.

Don't you understand that?"

"I didn't mean to hurt you, Elle," Merlin said, "but I'd do anything for Maggie."

"But why did your deathless love have to be kept a secret?" Laurette asked.

"Maggie thought it wouldn't look good for Curt's campaign if his manager was dating the opponent," Merlin said, "so she said no one could know."

"But I could tell everyone now," Elle said. "The last debate is tomorrow. I could totally out you."

"Yes, I guess you could," Merlin said. He looked sad.

"Merlin, you idiot, she's using you," Laurette said. "You have access to the perfect spying spot. That's why she's pretending to be your girlfriend."

Merlin looked stricken. "Do you really think she's pretending?"

"Sure," Laurette said. "It makes so much sense."

"Laurette, you don't know that," Elle said. "I think you're wrong." Turning to Merlin, she added, "I think Maggie really likes you."

"You do?" He perked up a bit. "I have to admit, it bothered me that she didn't want anyone to know. She said it was because of the election, but I thought if she really liked me . . ."

"She really likes you, Merlin," Elle said. "I know she does. She's just trying to have things both ways—win the election and have you, too."

"That lying, sneaky pinch-face," Laurette said. "We can't let her get away with this. We've got one day to get ready for that debate—and we're going to blow you and Curt away, Merlin. Everybody in school will vote for Elle. And we're not going to let *you* know what we're up to. This time it's going to be a surprise."

"Yeah, our campaign headquarters is off limits now," Elle said. "You kind of ruined it for us, Merlin."

"I'm sorry," Merlin said. "Just don't tell Maggie on me. Please? I don't know what she'll do."

"I'd be worried if I were you, too," Laurette said. "I don't know what we're going to do. But if it were up to me, protecting your relationship with Maggie wouldn't be a main concern."

"But we'll try not to make her mad at you," Elle said.

"Elle! Where's your killer instinct?" Laurette said. "Your political savvy? Your need to win at any cost?"

"I don't have any of those things," Elle said. "I just want to make sure my last two years of high school involve dances. For that, I'll sacrifice almost anything."

"That's her version of killer instinct," Laurette said. "It's unconventional, but it works."

"There's one more mystery we haven't solved," Elle said. "Who is Deep Ghost?"

"Deep Ghost?" Merlin said. "Never heard of him."

"He—or she—is someone who tried to help me," Elle said. "Without Deep Ghost I wouldn't have known to look for the gold paint on your fingers as a sign of your guilt. You could have told me you were in here painting your tuba and I would have thought nothing of it. I would have believed you."

"But I *was* in here painting my tuba," Merlin said.

"Yes, but that's not all you were doing," Laurette said.

"Today it was," Merlin said. "I wasn't expecting you to show up to plot and scheme until tomorrow."

"Whatever," Elle said. "We caught you just in time, and it's partly thanks to a brave soul named Deep Ghost."

"Maybe he wishes to remain anonymous," Laurette said.

"Perhaps," Elle said. "But I hope to find him or her or it and thank him, or her, or it, somehow."

★ ★ ★

Elle sat in her room that night, working on her speech. It was the most important speech of her campaign, her last chance to win over the voters. But she was struggling with it. What could she say that she hadn't said already?

She had a hard time keeping her mind on politics. All she could think about was Hunter.

Someone tapped lightly on her door. Probably Bernard, she thought, bringing her snacks. "Come in," she said.

The door opened. "Hey, there. Thought I'd surprise you." It was Hunter!

She jumped up and ran to him. She hadn't seen him in so long! He smelled good, like paper and ink and leather.

"All ready for the election, Miss President?" he asked. He peered at her laptop to read her speech, but the screen was blank.

"No," she said. "I can't concentrate. I keep thinking about this Saturday."

"This Saturday?" Hunter said. "What's this Saturday?"

"Homecoming, silly," Elle said. "I didn't think I'd get to see you until the dance."

"Oh, no," Hunter said. "The dance is Saturday night?"

Elle nodded. She didn't like the look on his face.

"I thought it was next week," he said. "I don't know how I got so mixed up."

"Is there a problem?" Elle asked.

He sat down on the bed and took her hands in his. "I've got a huge lab report due Monday," he told her. "And my lab partner and I have to work all weekend on it. We're studying a rat's behavior over the course of forty-eight hours. Someone has to be there to watch it every minute. I promised my partner I'd take the night shift."

"On Saturday night?" Elle asked.

Hunter nodded. "I'm so sorry, Elle. But this project counts as eighty percent of my grade." He squeezed her hands to show her how sorry he was.

"It's okay." She sat down next to him. She knew how important this was to him, and she didn't want him to feel bad about it. But the dance wouldn't be the same without him. Not even close. "Homecoming isn't a big deal."

"It *is* a big deal," Hunter said. "But not as big as Prom. That's the mother of all dances. And I promise, nothing will keep me away from that. It will be the anniversary of our very first date."

She smiled and felt a little better. He was right—they'd always have Prom.

"I'll make it up to you," he added. "I'll take you out to dinner. We'll celebrate your victory!"

"If I win," Elle said, glancing at her blank laptop.

"Having trouble with your speech?" Hunter asked.

Elle nodded. "I can't think of anything new to say."

"You know what angle you haven't tried yet?" Hunter said. "Show them your real self. Speak from the heart. If you do that, how will anyone be able to resist you?"

He hugged her, and she hugged him back. It was good advice. And besides, she didn't have much choice. She had run out of ideas.

"I'll try it," she said. "I'll just be myself. If they don't like me, they don't like me."

"That's impossible," Hunter said.

It was good to see him again. They kissed and kissed until someone knocked on the door. This time it *was* Bernard, with snacks.

"I'd better get going," Hunter said. "Good luck tomorrow. And I'm sorry again about the dance."

"I'm sorry, too," Elle said. But as he was leaving, an idea occurred to her. It was too bad Hunter couldn't take her to the dance, but there might be a way to make the best of it.

Chapter 19

I've got a friend, her name is Elle.
She's got no secret agenda to sell.
All she wants is harmony, cool,
Justice, truth, and dancing at school.
She wants what you want, think it through.
So, vote for Elle, She's your friend, too.
Vote Blonde!

"That song is so beautiful." Elle struggled not to cry the first time Laurette played it for her on her guitar. "It's so sweet! Thank you. I know it will help."

"You're welcome," Laurette said. "You've worked hard on this campaign. I hope the best girl wins."

Laurette had recorded the campaign song for

Elle, and it played through the school PA system all day on Thursday, the final debate day. It alternated with a flashy Vote Curt ad ("Vote for Curt unless you want to get hurt—just kidding—not."), a tuba rendition of "I Believe I Can Fly," by guess who—Merlin—and several Homecoming Queen jingles:

"Classy, not tacky; pretty, not showy; the quality choice is cheerleader Chloe!"

"Chessie Morton is my name; I want to be your Queenie; vote for me for Homecoming or you're a rotten meanie." (This was sung to the tune of *Yankee Doodle.*)

Then came a tuba rendition of "Yes! We Have No Bananas" (Merlin again).

"I can't figure out what that song has to do with Homecoming," Elle said to Laurette, who shrugged and said that Merlin's mind worked in mysterious ways.

There were also several bad songs in support of Jessica, Anna, and Kyra. Chris Rodriguez didn't even bother making an ad. He just assumed the Homecoming King's crown was his.

"The campaign for president has been very, uh, *lively* this year," Ms. Mikulski said as she stood on the left side of the stage, moderating the final presidential debate. The three candidates stood behind podiums lined up on the right. "So I want to keep today's debate as civilized and orderly as possible. I would like to ask each candidate this question: what is your main campaign promise? And how do you propose to keep it? Let's start with you, Merlin. I believe your slogan is 'Merlin and his tuba—two for the price of one.' Is that correct?"

"Yes, it is," Merlin said.

"Remind us of your main campaign promise, please."

"If elected president, I promise to serenade the school on my tuba every day." Merlin held up the golden horn as if he were introducing it to the audience, which was unnecessary; they all knew it only too well. There was a collective groan. Elle couldn't help noticing that Merlin still had gold paint on his fingers.

"No need to fulfill that promise yet, Merlin," Ms. Mikulski said. "Not until you've been elected."

Elle imagined what everyone was probably thinking: *which will never happen, thank God.*

"Okay," Merlin said. "But I think it's pretty obvious how I'll keep that promise—and that I can."

"Spare us," someone yelled from the audience.

"Thank you, Merlin," the principal said. "Curt?"

"Thank you, Ms. Mikulski," Curt said, flashing a grin at the principal. "I've made many promises in my campaign: the elimination of rope-climbing from all gym classes; the hiring of more Latin teachers— our classics department is woefully ill staffed; and the addition of a magazine rack in the cafeteria, so that those who have no one to eat with will have something to read—to name just a few.

"But my main promise is: no more school dances. Think about it. How many times have you looked at your calendar, seen that a dance was coming up, and felt a chill? A creeping sense of dread?" He paused dramatically.

"For many students at Beverly Hills, the only purpose dances serve is as a reminder that no one of the opposite sex likes them. I'm being very frank here. Brutally honest. And for those who have dates, what do they need a dance for? They can go out together wherever they want. All a dance provides is nosy teachers for chaperones, trying to suss out whether or not you've been drinking or if you're hiding cigarettes in your jacket. That's why I say: get rid of them. They're outdated. Old-fashioned. We need to come up with new ways to socialize. Ways that don't involve pain, loneliness, and humiliation. Thank you."

The crowd stirred. Some people cheered, some jeered. Elle thought the jeers outnumbered the cheers—she hoped so.

"And how will you keep this promise, Curt?" Ms. Mikulski asked.

"Easy," Curt said. "One swipe of the pen. Canceled. All dances off. Think of all the weekend nights you'll have freed up."

A small section of the auditorium raucously yelled their approval. They waved a sign reading, DATELESS WONDERS FOR CURT. Another sign said, DANCES ARE A VIOLATION OF MY CIVIL RIGHTS.

Elle's nerves were jangled. She had her work cut out for her.

"All right, calm down, everybody," Ms. Mikulski said. "Elle Woods, what is your promise?"

"I promise to find a date for every student for every dance," Elle said. "As long as I'm student body president, no one will go without a date if they want one."

Elle's cheering section, led by the cheerleaders (who were, after all, experts at it), shouted their approval. Her signs said, SHE CAN DO IT—I BELIEVE! and A VOTE FOR ELLE IS A VOTE FOR YOUR SOCIAL LIFE.

"I don't understand why Curt hates dances so much," Elle said. "I know it hurts when you don't

164

have a date. But it doesn't have to be that way. Everyone can have fun at a dance, even people who don't have dates. But if you feel better going with someone, all you have to do is ask the person.

"You can't abolish dances. That's like getting rid of football games, and first-day-of-school jitters, and school plays. It's a tradition. It's part of life. And it can be beautiful."

The audience was quiet. Elle's confidence surged, and her voice got stronger. Hunter was right: being herself was the best way to reach people.

"I have a story to tell," she said. "Last year, I was a mousy girl in glasses, braces, and baggy clothes. No one noticed me. I bet most of you didn't even know I was alive. And I wasn't happy. I wasn't myself. I was hiding the real blonde fashion plate who lived inside me, struggling to get out.

"What happened? How did I get from there to here, standing before the entire school, asking for your vote?

"Something inspired me. Something pushed me to let my inner blonde out, to blossom into my true self. And that something was the mother of all dances, the Senior Prom."

The crowd murmured. The cheerleaders waved their Vote Elle signs in encouragement.

"To go to Prom with the boy that I liked was my dream," Elle continued. "It inspired me to change everything about myself, from the way I look to the way I act. Working toward that goal forced me to come out of my shell. As most of you know, I went to Prom with the guy who is now my boyfriend. And it was the greatest night of my life.

"Sometimes I think: What if there were no dances? No Prom? That night would never have happened. And I wouldn't be standing before you now, a reformed 'mouseburger' with a whole new life."

The cheerleaders clapped and whistled. Some of the other students joined in. Elle could feel that the audience was with her.

"Without dances, high school is just a lot of tests and bad food. Beverly Hills High needs its dances. Don't get rid of them. It would be a huge mistake. Thank you."

"That's a lovely sentiment, Elle," Ms. Mikulski said. "But how on earth do you propose to keep that promise? To find a date for every single student?"

"All it takes is a little empathy," Elle said. "If you watch people carefully, you start to notice things about them. I can tell when people like each other—even when they don't want to admit it. I see couples the way that kid in *The Sixth Sense* saw dead people."

"It's a lie!" one of Curt's geeks shouted.

"Yeah, prove it!" another one yelled.

"All right," Elle said. "The Homecoming Dance is the first one of the year. It's Saturday night. A lot of you don't have dates because everyone assumes that Curt will be reelected, which means there won't be a dance. But what if he loses? If I win, or even if Merlin does, the Homecoming Dance will go on as scheduled. It will be one of the big events of the year. And then what will you do? You can go alone, of course. But isn't it more fun to go with someone you like?"

One of Curt's geeks, a boy named Alan, waved his hand. "Pick me, pick me!"

"Okay, Alan." Elle scanned the crowd, looking for a girl who would be willing to go to the dance with a boy whose idea of a good time was staring at stamps under a magnifying glass in search of valuable flaws. Aha—there she was. Tiina Jervaarts, an exchange student from Finland, who got lots of letters from home covered in exotic stamps. Also, she didn't speak English very well, so if Alan said a lot of boring things to her, she wouldn't notice.

"How about Tiina?" Elle said. "Tiina, what do you say?"

"*Vat*? I don't understand," Tiina said.

The girl sitting next to her, her host student, explained the situation.

"Oh? Yes! I want to go to the dance," Tiina said.

"Alan?" Elle said. "What do you say? She's a cutie."

Alan beamed and then cowered under Curt's disapproving glare. "Well, there won't *be* a dance, but if there were, sure, I'd go with Tiina."

"Good," Elle said. "Then it's all settled. Let's try another one." Elle felt the pain of Chessie's unrequited love for Chris and wanted to do something to help her. And she had a hunch she could.

At that moment, Jessica McMartin—Chris's ex— was the front-runner for Homecoming Queen. And traditionally (Elle had researched the rules), the King and Queen went to the dance together . . . *unless* one or both of them already had dates. In which case, the King and Queen had one dance together but were allowed to spend the rest of the evening with their true dates.

Elle had a feeling that going to a dance with Jessica was Chris's worst nightmare come true. They hadn't spoken to each other in months.

"Chessie Morton," Elle said. "Do you need a date to the dance?"

Chessie looked nervous, and Elle understood why. She didn't want to be matched with one of Curt's geeky friends. She had her heart set on one particular date.

"Kind of," Chessie said. "But that's okay, Elle. No need to work your special brand of magic on me."

"Chessie, trust me," Elle said. "Chris Rodriguez? Will you take Chessie to Homecoming?"

Chris, who'd been caught up in a PlayStation game and not paying attention, looked up, startled, at the sound of his name. "Huh?"

"Hey, that doesn't count," a girl yelled. It was probably a girl who, like Chessie, had had her eye on Chris. "They're both running for King and Queen, so they might go together anyway."

"That's true," Elle said. "But what if one of them doesn't win? What if neither one wins? They'll still need a date. And they might as well go with some-one they like instead of someone the people elected them to be with."

"That's for sure," Chris said. "Who did you say you matched me with?"

"Chessie Morton."

"Uh, which one is she again?" Chris stood up

and scanned the crowd from back to front.

Chessie sprang to her feet. "Here I am! Me! Me! Ow!" While jumping up and down in excitement she kicked over a metal chair.

"Yeah, sure. That's cool," Chris said. "She's a cheerleader, so that's decent."

"Great!" Elle said. Chessie was glowing with happiness. "So you see, anyone who needs help with a date, I'm here for you."

"Wait a minute," Curt said. "How do we know these people weren't planted by you in the audience?"

"Hey, that's right," Merlin said. "Why don't you take on a real challenge? Find a date for me."

Elle, surprised, couldn't help turning toward Maggie, standing backstage as Curt's manager. Her pinched face looked hard and extra-pinched. *Interesting,* Elle thought. What was Merlin doing? Was he trying to force Maggie to admit that she liked him in public? Was he testing her?

"Wait a second, Elle," Curt said with false friendliness. "I know you mean well and want to help out the socially less fortunate. But some people are just complete lost causes. Hopeless cases. It's for those people that I'm running. The people that no one can save. And I'm afraid Mr. Tuba here is one of those people. He's not just one of them—he is their king: King Merlin, the Unmatchable."

Merlin looked hurt by Curt's words, and Elle didn't blame him. "You're wrong, Curt," she said. "Merlin isn't hard to match at all. I know the perfect girl for him, and I'd bet anything she'll say yes."

The crowd got rowdy, shouting for one side or the other, daring Elle to match Merlin the Unmatchable with a living, breathing female.

"But first, let me ask you, the students of Beverly Hills High," Elle said. "Do you believe I can do it?"

A chorus of yeahs and nos flew at her. She thought she heard more yeahs, but it was hard to tell.

"All right, tell me this," she said. "If I do this—if I find a girl who wants to go to the dance with Merlin—and this is not a setup—after all, he is my opponent and has no motivation to help me out— if I do this, will you vote for me and keep dances alive at Beverly Hills?"

"YES!!!" the roar came back to her.

"Okay," Elle said. She took a deep breath, because she knew Maggie held all the cards here. She had the power to burn Elle, and good reason to. Her saying yes would hurt Curt's chances. All she had to do was say no to Merlin in front of the whole school. It would be easy for her, especially if she was as much of an opportunist as she sometimes appeared to be.

But Elle didn't think she was. Deep down, Elle thought, Pinch-face was a softy, at least when it came to Merlin.

Merlin was shaking like a nervous puppy. His adoration of Maggie was written all over his face. How could a pinch-face say no to a puppy-face like that?

"All right, Merlin," Elle said. "I have the perfect date for you. Maggie Licht, will you please step on to the stage?"

Maggie walked out from backstage, her face more pinched than ever.

"Merlin, would you like to go to the dance with Maggie?" Elle asked.

Merlin nodded vigorously. "Yes. More than I want to be Homecoming King. More than I want to be student body president. More than I want to play tuba in the marching band. More than I've ever wanted anything in my life."

The crowd roared. Maggie looked stricken by his confession. She hadn't been expecting it. She had probably thought Merlin would play along with their charade. That was her mistake.

"Maggie, what about you?" Elle asked. "Will you go to the dance with Merlin?"

"Yes! Yes! Yes! Yes!" the crowd chanted, totally into the drama. Curt scowled.

Maggie pinched up her face tighter than ever. She looked at Curt, who shook his head and whispered, "No," though no one could hear it over the noise.

Then she looked at Elle, who tried to keep her expression neutral. Maggie's sharp eyes glared angrily at her for putting her in such a position.

Finally, Maggie looked at Merlin, whose crumpled smile and round Charlie Brown head were pathetic and irresistible. At last her face softened. Maggie looked like a different person when faced with Merlin's sad, pleading smile.

"Say yes! Say yes!" the crowd chanted.

"Well, Maggie?" Elle asked. "The crowd is dying to know. Will you go to the Homecoming Dance with Merlin the Unmatchable?"

The chanting stopped. A hush fell over the room as everyone waited for her answer.

"He's not unmatchable," Maggie said. "I'd love to go out with him."

The crowd nearly blew the roof off the auditorium. They went crazy with cheering and laughing.

All, that is, except for Curt, who looked glum.

Merlin hugged Maggie, and after a moment's hesitation, she stiffly hugged him back. "I'm wild about this girl!" he told the crowd, and they cheered harder than ever.

Ms. Mikulski clapped and cheered, too, for a few minutes, before returning to her role as principal and moderator. She banged her gavel. "Order! Order! Let's quiet down, people!"

But the kids started chanting, *"Merlin and Maggie! Merlin and Maggie! Elle! Elle! Elle! Elle! Hooray!"*

"This concludes our final debate," Ms. Mikulski shouted into her microphone. "Don't forget to go to the polls tomorrow and vote!"

Chapter 20

"I SAID I'd go out with Merlin," Maggie told a reporter from the school newspaper. She and Merlin were surrounded by a crowd of students after the debate. "I didn't say I'd go to the dance."

"But will you?" the reporter asked. "If there is a dance?"

"*If* there's a dance," Maggie said. "But there won't be a dance. I still think everybody should vote for Curt. He's the best candidate."

"Hey, what about me?" Merlin said. "I'm running for president, too."

Maggie squeezed his chubby cheeks together. "You're the best *tuba player*. And I like you the best as a person. But I'm still Curt's campaign manager."

Merlin grinned. "I can't wait for this election to be over."

"How can she be so two-faced?" Elle whispered to Laurette. "Holding hands with Merlin while she tells everyone to vote for Curt?"

"And he just stands there smiling like an idiot," Laurette said. "She'll make a good politician someday."

"And he'll be the perfect political spouse," Elle said. "Smiling and quiet and agreeable."

"So what I'm saying is," Maggie continued, "it doesn't matter whether there's a dance or not. If there isn't, Merlin and I will go out on our own. We don't need a school dance to validate our love."

"Ick," Laurette said.

"She so totally doesn't get it," Elle said. "After all the love that filled that auditorium, all the cheering and chanting for them . . . she's still antidance?"

"What about you, Elle?" The reporter turned to her, tape recorder in hand. "How do you feel, now that the last debate is over? You made a big splash in there."

"I'm feeling great," Elle said. "Now that the halls of Beverly Hills High are filled with love, I know that the students will want to keep the tradition of school dances alive. A vote for me is a vote for love. Vote Blonde!"

"You've narrowed Curt's lead by a lot," the reporter said. "Still, the polls are close. What are you going to do to swing the election in your favor tomorrow?"

"There's not much I can do now," Elle said. "Just hope things go my way."

The reporter went off to interview Curt. The school day was over. There was one more thing Elle wanted to do: find out the identity of Deep Ghost.

"I'm feeling spooky," she said to Laurette. "Want to take a walk through the Haunted House?"

"Let's go," Laurette said.

The Haunted House had just opened for the day. The younger children who usually thronged the place hadn't arrived from school yet. It was the perfect time to go ghost hunting.

Elle and Laurette paid the entrance fee and walked in. Elle was used to the spiderwebs, the spinning hallways, and the gross-out scenes by then. She walked about halfway through the house and stopped in the Chamber of Horrors. Deep Ghost seemed to haunt that area regularly.

"Deep Ghost? Are you here?" Elle called.

"Anybody undead home?" Laurette said.

The house was noisy with the usual screams, creaks, evil laughs, and spooky organ music.

"Boooo . . ." Elle heard the familiar electronic voice of Deep Ghost. The phantom stepped out of the shadows, arms raised high, trying to scare them. "Enter the Chamber of Horrors . . . if you dare," Deep Ghost growled.

"That's him?" Laurette said. She reached for the ghost's sheet and tried to tug it off. Deep Ghost darted away.

"How dare you!" the voice boomed. "You cannot know the undead! For that you must be punished!"

"I can't tell if it's a boy or a girl," Laurette said.

"I know," Elle said. "It's that weird voice changer. It makes him sound like the killer in *Scream*."

"Yeah, exactly," Laurette said. "That's exactly who he sounds like."

"Stop talking about me like I'm not right here in front of you!" the ghost commanded.

"That machine can make anything sound spooky," Laurette said. "Hey, Ghost—say, 'Gag me with a spoon.'"

"No," the ghost said.

"Aw, come on," Elle said.

"Gag me with a spoon!" the ghost boomed.

Elle and Laurette laughed.

"Stop laughing at me!" the ghost said. "I'm trying to terrify you! This is serious."

"That's really funny," Elle said.

"His voice is starting to sound different," Laurette said. "Kind of wobbly."

"Stop calling me 'he,'" Deep Ghost said. "I'm not a—I mean, I'm not a he or a she, I'm a genderless spirit."

That really cracked Elle and Laurette up. "So what should we call you, 'It'?" Laurette said.

"Cousin Itt," Elle said.

"Just pass through the Chamber of Horrors and leave me alone," Deep Ghost said. "You're holding up the line."

The volume of the ghost's voice began to shift up and down, as if the microphone's batteries were losing power.

"There's nobody behind us yet," Laurette said. She leaned down. "Can you see its shoes? Maybe we can tell who it is that way."

The ghost squatted to make sure its sheet covered its shoes. "You guys, cut it out," it said in a slightly different voice. The voice changer was definitely losing power. Deep Ghost now sounded distinctly feminine—no question about it.

"It's a girl," Elle said.

"I am not a girl," Deep Ghost said in a high-pitched voice, stamping its feet. "Why isn't this thing working?" The ghost tripped over its sheet and tumbled to the floor. "Ow!" it said in a whiny voice.

"It's Chessie!" Elle and Laurette said at the same time.

"No! Not Chessie!" the ghost said. "Boo! Go away!"

It was so totally Chessie.

"Chessie, I want to kiss you!" Elle said. "You helped me so much."

Defeated, Chessie pulled off her sheet and sat down on a tombstone. "I was wearing a disguise for a reason, you know."

"I'd never believe it if I hadn't seen it with my own eyes," Laurette said. "Why did you go to so much trouble to help Elle? That's not like you."

"Well it wasn't for your sake, that's for sure, Laurette," Chessie said.

Elle sat down beside Chessie. "I know why you helped me. It was because of the Cheerleader's Oath, wasn't it?"

"The what? No," Chessie said. "It was because I like dances as much as you do. I really don't care if you're school president or not. I just didn't want Curt to get rid of the dances. Especially if I'm going to be Homecoming Queen. What good is being Homecoming Queen if there's no dance? When will I get to be all queeny and lord it over everybody?"

"There's the football game," Laurette said. "And the halftime parade."

"That's not enough," Chessie said. "I need a dance. With starlight and strobes and romantic music and a handsome boy—"

"I totally agree with you," Elle said. "But how did you know Merlin was spying on us?"

"It was an accident," Chessie said. "You know how Maggie's always on her cell?"

Elle nodded. Maggie did always have her cell phone with her.

"Well she called me to ask me if I would spy on you," Chessie said. "I said no—mostly because I just didn't feel like it. But I could have said yes easily, so I hope you appreciate it—"

"I do appreciate it," Elle said. "Really."

"But I also said no, because, obviously, I don't want Curt to win, because I like dances," Chessie said.

"We get that," Laurette said.

"So, anyway, I guess Maggie sat on her phone by accident and pressed REDIAL and didn't know it," Chessie said. "So her phone called me, and I could hear her talking. She was talking to Merlin—and he was telling her about the vent in the band equipment room."

"What a sneak," Laurette said.

"Later I saw Merlin coming out of the equipment room after one of our powwows," Chessie said. "I knew what he was up to. He must have told Maggie that I spotted him. So she threatened me—she said if I told anybody she'd sabotage my chances of becoming Homecoming Queen. She said she'd do an even worse hatchet job on me that she was doing on you. Spreading rumors, taping mean signs on my back . . . the whole bit."

"Chessie, that's awful," Elle said.

"I *know,*" Chessie said. "I mean, you haven't got much to lose—your chances of winning the election are pretty slim. But me—imagine *me* not being Homecoming Queen. It's a catastrophe!"

"A tragedy," Laurette said. "Imagine a non–Chessie Homecoming Queen. How did the school ever survive it before?"

"I guess it just means that all Homecomings were lame until this one," Chessie said, completely missing Laurette's sarcastic tone—as usual.

"Wait—can we go back to the Deep Ghost thing again?" Elle said. "I still don't understand why you wanted me to meet you here. If Maggie had caught you, she could have smeared your rep. Why did you do it?"

"I already told you," Chessie said. "I want you to win so we can have dances. But I had to keep Maggie from finding out that I was helping you, or she'd have started trashing me. That's why I had to be anonymous—or my Homecoming career would have been over. So you won't tell, will you? Promise?"

"I swear on the Cheerleader's Oath," Elle said.

"Er, okay, I guess that works," Chessie said. "But what about her?" She jerked her head at Laurette. "She's not a cheerleader."

"I swear on the honor code of the Thrift-Store Shoppers of America," Laurette said.

"And what's that?" Chessie asked.

"Dry-clean it and it's good as new!" Laurette said.

"Elle," Chessie said. "Make her swear on something real."

"She won't tell," Elle said. "She's the most trustworthy person I know. And besides, revealing your identity would only hurt our chances tomorrow. So don't worry, your secret is safe."

"Thank you. Now please leave before somebody comes and finds us," Chessie said.

Elle and Laurette got to their feet. "Good luck tomorrow, Chessie," Elle said. "I'll vote for you. But don't tell Chloe."

"I'll vote for you, too, Elle," Chessie said. "Even though everybody says you're too spacey to be president. Whenever they say that, I always defend you. I always say you're spacey in a good way."

"Thanks, Chessie," Elle said. She was genuinely touched.

Chapter 21

"ELLE, YOU'RE not eating your sesame-crusted ahi fillet," Elle's mother, Eva, complained.

"Or your tomato soup with lobster," her father, Wyatt, added. "What's the matter? Don't you like it?"

"The food here is so good I don't mind breaking my diet," Eva said. She changed diets often, as the fads dictated. This week she was on the Rodent Diet. Basically, she could only eat cheese, nuts, lettuce, and so on—whatever a rabbit, mouse, squirrel, rat, or other rodent would eat. Fish and lobster weren't allowed.

With a fork, Elle poked at a bit of lobster. Her parents had taken her out to dinner at Plexus, the latest hot restaurant, to take her mind off the election. It wasn't working. "I'm nervous, I guess," she said.

"Because of that silly election tomorrow?" Eva asked. "Darling, I had no idea you were so *political*." She shuddered, as if the word tasted bitter on her tongue.

"She's not political," Wyatt said. "She's just competitive, like me. Right, pussycat? She likes to win."

"You're both wrong," Elle said.

"Elle, please," Eva said, "we're your parents. When it comes to you, we're never wrong."

Elle let that glaringly false statement pass. "It's not that I care about winning or school politics so much. It's the Homecoming Dance. And every other dance this year. Even though Hunter isn't around to take me, I really want to go."

"Of course you do, darling. Who wouldn't?" Eva said.

"Is that what all the fuss has been about these past few weeks?" Wyatt said.

"Yes, Daddy," Elle said. "I ran for president to save school dances from extinction."

"Well, I had no idea." Wyatt dipped his bread in extra-extra-virgin olive oil and chewed thoughtfully.

"Yes, you did, Wyatt," Eva said, rolling her eyes. "You knew; you just forgot. You got all caught up in the hospital tennis tournament—"

Elle wished dinner would end so she could go home and pace nervously in her room, maybe make a few last–minute "Vote Blonde" phone calls to key constituents. The brainiacs were pretty much lost to Curt, and the band geeks to Merlin, but she thought she could sway a few apathetic social types to vote for her.

Elle's cell phone beeped. "It's Hunter," she said.

"You must take it," Eva said. She loved Hunter. "We'll excuse you."

Elle went outside to take the call.

"Just wanted to wish you good luck one more time," Hunter said.

"Thanks," Elle said.

"And I was thinking about the dance," Hunter said. "It kills me that I can't go with you. But if you want to ask someone else, I'll understand. Just as friends, of course. I'd hate for you to have to go without a date."

"There's no one else I'd want to go with," Elle said. But that wasn't quite true. Maybe there *was* someone else she'd like to go with. Not in a romantic way, but for a different reason . . .

Eva looked up when she returned to the table. "What did Hunter have to say?"

"Just 'Good luck,'" Elle said.

"What a sweetheart," Eva said. "Are you still feeling nervous?"

"A little," Elle said.

"I know what will cheer you up," Wyatt said. "A nice big ice-cream sundae."

"Darling, they don't serve those here," Eva said. "Unless it's garlic ice cream with whipped parsley essence."

"Well," Wyatt said. "That's not going to cheer anyone up, is it?"

"It's okay," Elle said. "I'm beyond the ice-cream-cheer-up stage. If we could just get out of here—"

"Of course, pussycat," Wyatt said, summoning the waiter. "We'll go home and have a nice, quiet evening. Sit around. Mope. Bite our nails. Maybe even play a game of Monopoly. What do you say?"

"Oh, Wyatt," Eva said. "We don't want to bore the poor girl to death."

When they pulled into the driveway, the house was dark except for a light in the kitchen. "Bernard and Zosia must have gone to bed already," Wyatt said.

"But it's only nine o'clock," Elle said. That didn't sound like Bernard, or Zosia, who liked to stay up late and watch the talk shows.

"What are you going to do?" Wyatt said. "Help just isn't any fun anymore."

They walked into the house. Eva flicked on the light.

"Surprise!"

Elle jumped back in shock. Her father caught her and propped her up by holding her elbows.

The room was packed with people: Laurette, Chessie, all the other cheerleaders, a few other friends, and Zosia and Bernard. Over their heads hung a big yellow banner that said, VOTE BLONDE ELECTION EVE PHONE-ATHON.

"Wow," Elle said. "What is this?"

"It was Laurette's idea," Eva said.

"We all came over to call everyone in school and make sure they know to vote for you," Laurette said.

"We'll do anything to help," Zosia said. "Bribe them, threaten them . . ."

"I don't think that's legal," Elle said.

"It isn't?" Zosia said.

"We'll just *urge* them to vote," Tamila, one of the freshman cheerleaders, said.

"And I might mention the hot race for Homecoming Queen, while I've got them on the phone," Chessie said.

Chloe threw her an angry glance. The Homecoming competition was heating up. "We're here to help Elle, not ourselves," she snapped.

"Oh, like you won't totally push them to vote for you," Chessie said.

"Girls, girls, let's not have fighting," Laurette said. "Let's face it, you're both losers. Jessica McMartin is practically wearing the crown already. All right, everybody. Let's hit those phones!"

Bernard had set up tables in the living room with a school directory at each place. He served snacks and drinks while the guests made their calls. Soon the room was full of chatter.

"Elle, over here!" Lisi, the other freshman cheerleader, called from the couch. "I've got someone on the line who needs some extra convincing."

Elle took the phone from her. "This is Elle Woods, candidate for president. Who's this?"

"Elle, it's Sidney. What's going on over there? Are you having a party?"

"No, it's a phone-athon. I thought you needed some convincing to vote for me. Do you?"

"I'll vote for you if you go to the dance with me," Sidney said.

"Sorry, but I already have a date in mind," Elle said.

"You mean you haven't been asked yet?" Sidney said.

"No. But I'm pretty sure the guy I'm thinking of is available."

"What if he isn't? Then will you go with me?"

"Sidney, just vote for me. As a friend."

"Okay," Sidney said. "But don't tell Merlin."

"I won't. Do you want to come over and help with the phone-athon?" She was nervous about asking him, since she was afraid he might drive away more voters than he brought in. But it wasn't possible to smell bologna over the telephone, so she figured it was probably safe.

"Sidney? Are you there?"

He seemed to have dropped the phone. Someone knocked on the glass sliding door that led to the terrace. He'd run over from next door without waiting to be asked again.

"Sidney! How's your father?" Wyatt said, showing him to a chair. "Sit down and start dialing. Can I get you some lemonade?"

Elle listened to the swell of voices around her. It made her feel good to think that all those people were willing to give up a Thursday night—which everyone knew was the cool night to go out, the weekend being for amateurs—just to help her.

"Hi, I'm P. J. Stoller, calling to remind you to vote for Elle Woods for president tomorrow. Keep dances alive! Vote Blonde!"

"Hi, I'm calling from Elle Woods campaign headquarters," Chessie said. "Hear all that noise in the background? It's totally happening here. All the cool people in school got together to tell the rest of you to vote for Elle. No, of course I didn't mean *you*. I meant everybody else at school. And don't forget about Homecoming Queen. The cool vote is Chris for King and Chessie for Queen. What do you mean, you don't like her? She's a doll! Hey, stop saying that! Yeah? Well, same to you, jerk!"

"Chessie, what are you trying to do, alienate the whole school?" Laurette said.

"You should have heard what that guy said about me," Chessie said.

Elle had a special call to make. She looked up the number in the school directory and dialed.

A boy answered. "Curt Blaylock speaking."

"Curt, this is Elle."

"Ah. Have you called to concede already? The election isn't until tomorrow."

"I'm not calling to concede," Elle said. "I'm calling to tell you that if I win the election, you won't have to worry about finding a date for the Homecoming

Dance. If you want one, you've got one."

"Oh? And what desperate girl have you got who's willing to go with the loser? Which, I hate to tell you, I *won't* be."

"Me," Elle said.

There was silence on the other end. Then Curt said, "You? You'd be willing to go to the dance with me? You, the cute, blonde, popular captain of the cheerleaders?"

"Yes, Curt, I would," Elle said. "It would be an honor. Do you accept?"

"I don't know what to say."

"Say yes."

There was another silence.

"Curt?"

"No," Curt said. "I can't say yes. I don't need a date, because there won't be a dance. Because I'm going to win. Do you hear me? I'm going to win."

He sounded very certain, but she didn't let it faze her.

"All right, Curt," she said. "I'll see you tomorrow. And may the best candidate win."

He hung up. *He needs a dance more than anybody,* she thought. If only he would realize it.

Chapter 22

"REMEMBER, NO campaigning within twenty feet of the polling station!" Mr. Wrightsman said. Merlin was marching through the halls playing his tuba, and had gotten too close to the voting tables. Mr. Wrightsman shooed him away.

"I'm not campaigning," Merlin said. "I'm just playing music."

"Please, Merlin," Mr. Wrightsman said. "We all know your agenda by now: all tuba, all the time. Twenty feet. Shoo. Don't worry, the music carries."

Kids mobbed the two voting tables on Friday morning, election day. Each table had a large cardboard box on it, sealed, with a slit in the middle and lots of slips of paper and pens. One was marked

HOMECOMING and the other PRESIDENT. Ms. Mikulski manned the presidential table and Mr. Wrightsman the one for Homecoming. They checked off students' names as they voted to make sure no one voted twice. But it wasn't easy to keep track of the crowd. So many kids wanted to vote that they pushed and shoved against the tables.

The phone-athon had worked, at least in stimulating a good turnout. Elle was amazed. At the beginning of the school year most students had said they weren't going to bother to vote. They'd said that it didn't matter who the president was. Now, things were different. Elle had made it matter.

"You've got to stop campaigning sometime." Laurette took Elle by the arm and steered her toward the courtyard. "Come on, let's get away from the voting tables. It's a beautiful day. We've done all we could. It's out of our hands now."

"You're right," Elle said. They settled on the grass in a patch of sun. "But I'm still so nervous!"

"Me, too," Laurette said. "What can we do to distract ourselves?"

They soaked up the sun, thinking about it. The first-period bell rang.

"I guess we could go to class," Elle said.

"Yeah, maybe we should do that."

★ ★ ★

The polls closed at two-thirty, half an hour before the end of the school day. Ms. Mikulski and Mr. Wrightsman took the cardboard boxes into their offices and counted the votes.

Everyone was allowed to go home if he or she wanted to. Almost no one wanted to. Students gathered in the auditorium, where the announcements would be made, buzzing and talking and restlessly waiting for the results.

The counting seemed to take hours. "I can't stand this!" Chessie shrieked. She was pacing the aisles, kicking seats as she walked. "The waiting! I was never good at waiting."

"I know," Elle said. "They're taking forever."

"What are *you* so nervous about?" Chessie said. "You're just running for president! Big deal. I'm up for *Homecoming Queen*. Do you know how important that is? How huge? How life-changing?"

"Well, it really only lasts one day," P.J. said.

"That's not true," Chessie said. "It lasts for the rest of your life. If I win, I can always say I was a Homecoming Queen. I *am* a Homecoming Queen. I'll be entitled to wear a crown whenever I want to. Or a tiara, depending on which goes better with my outfit."

"You will?" Elle said. "I didn't know that. If I'd known about the crown thing, maybe I would have run for Queen, too."

"You can't walk around with a crown on your head for the rest of your life," Laurette said. "Trust me, nobody's going to let you get away with that."

"I'll pull it off somehow," Chessie said.

"Don't worry, Chessie," Elle said. "If you don't win this year, you can try again next year. So you'll still have a chance at that crown."

"No! I have to win this year!" Chessie's eyes were bloodshot, and she looked crazed, as if she'd just eaten a pound of white sugar, straight from the bag.

"Chill, Chessie," Laurette said. "You're losing it."

"It won't matter, anyway," Maggie said, interrupting them. "There won't be a Homecoming Dance, so being Queen won't mean much."

"Curt hasn't won yet," Laurette said.

"Doesn't that make you sad?" Elle said. "You were going to go to the dance with Merlin."

"It doesn't matter," Maggie said. "We're going to have our own dance. A private dance, so we can invite the people we like and keep out the people we don't like. A victory dance for Curt. It will be even better than a school dance."

"Sounds to me like there won't be that many

people in attendance," Laurette said.

"Only the people who count," Maggie said. "Our kind of people."

"Like I said," Laurette said.

There was a stir at the back of the room. Ms. Mikulski and Mr. Wrightsman marched up the center aisle to the stage. The students cleared a path for them, buzzing with suspense.

"Wow, quite a turnout," Ms. Mikulski said. "I never expected so many of you to stay after school voluntarily."

She paused for a laugh, but got only a small chuckle from the crowd.

"Moving on," she said. "I have the news you've all been waiting to hear. First, the results of the Homecoming election. For Homecoming King, by a margin of seventy percent to twenty-eight percent, two percent going to various write-in candidates named I. P. Freehly, Dewdrop Yerpantz, and Amanda Kissenhug, the winner is—Chris Rodriguez!"

The audience clapped loudly, though no one was surprised. Chris jumped onto the stage, took a quick bow, and jumped off again. He was surrounded by his friends, who immediately started teasing him and pretending to punch him in the face.

Elle was afraid Merlin would be disappointed, but his band buddies were patting him on the back, one of them saying, "You got twenty-eight percent of the votes! Way to go!"

And it was true. Elle was surprised that so many kids had voted for Merlin. It must have been a pity vote, she thought, from kids who knew he'd never win—or maybe a protest against Chris who, while nice enough, was an obvious choice.

"For Homecoming Queen, the race was very tight," Ms. Mikulski said, "but there was a winner, and she is—Chloe Gaitskill!"

The crowd applauded some more. Chloe jumped up and down, hugging her friends and squealing, "I did it! I did it!" The cheerleaders surrounded her, cheering. Chloe tried to hug Chessie, but Chessie pulled away.

"Don't be a bad sport, Chessie," Chloe said. "Remember—Cheerleader's Oath. We stick together, no matter what. It was a tough race."

"There's always next year," Elle said.

"You said that already," Chessie snapped.

"Who wants to walk around in a silly old crown anyway?" Laurette said.

"I do," Chessie said.

"But Chessie," Elle said. "You've already got the

best prize—the thing you wanted most of all. You're going to the Homecoming Dance with Chris. And he's the Homecoming King. So that's pretty much the same for you as being Homecoming Queen. And I'll bet he'll let you wear his crown."

"You still don't get it, do you?" Chessie said. "There isn't going to be a Homecoming Dance. So I won't get to be Chris's date after all."

"We'll see," Elle said, "in about five seconds."

"Congratulations to Chris and Chloe," Ms. Mikulski said. "Now, the race for president. The winner is, by a clear margin of twenty points—"

Elle held her breath. This was it. All her hard work came down to this moment.

"Sorry, I dropped my paper." A sheet of paper fluttered under the podium, and Ms. Mikulski bent down to retrieve it. Then she stood up, straightened her skirt, and cleared her throat.

"You'd think she wouldn't have to look at the piece of paper," Laurette said. "You'd think she'd know who won by heart."

"Guess she likes to be official," Elle said. Her heart was racing, and blood pounded in her ears. The next moment would decide what the rest of her high school life would be like—dance-free, or full of dances. And presidential decisions. And probably some meetings and paperwork.

"Okay, sorry about that," Ms. Mikulski said. "Your new president is—Elle Woods!"

A roar rose through the crowd. Everyone seemed surprised and happy. Elle stood perfectly still for a second, waiting for the news to sink in. Had she heard right? Was it real?

Laurette grabbed her and hugged her tight. "You won! You won!" she screamed.

It was real. She'd won!

"Hooray!" she cried, jumping up and down and accepting hugs and handshakes from everyone around her. Even Chessie looked pleased.

"Now I can go to the dance with Chris!" Chessie said. "Yay!"

"President Woods," Ms. Mikulski said, "would you like to come up and say a few words to your new constituency?"

Elle was practically tossed onto the stage by a sea of congratulating hands lifting her up and carrying her. Curt stood at the foot of the stage. He nodded at her, looking serious as usual.

"Congratulations," he said.

Ms. Mikulski stepped aside, and Elle took the podium.

"Thank you, everyone!" There were more cheers.

"I'm so happy to be president of this student body. Beverly Hills High is a wonderful school, and I'm going to work hard to make it even better."

"Hooray for Elle!" people shouted all around her.

"As you all know, this means that the Homecoming Dance—and every other dance scheduled for this year—is on! I hope you'll all be there!"

"Hooray!" The cheering got even louder.

"And remember—anyone who needs a date—you know where to go for help. The office of the president."

"Yay!"

"I'm very excited. I'd like to thank everyone who helped me, especially my loyal cheerleading squad, including this year's Homecoming Queen, Chloe Gaitskill. And Chessie Morton, who played a special role."

Chessie grinned, pleased with any attention she could get, however brief.

"And thanks to my campaign manager, Laurette Smythe. She did such a brilliant job. Without her I never could have won."

There were cheers for Laurette, who blew kisses to the crowd.

"And so many other people: my parents; my boyfriend, Hunter; my manicurist, Bibi Barbosa;

my maid, Zosia, and butler, Bernard; and all of my friends. And all of you who voted for me. Thank you! Give yourselves a hand!"

Much clapping followed.

"Most of all, I'd like to thank my opponents, Merlin Jones and Curt Blaylock. You were very tough to beat, but you always played fair. Pretty much. And now, as my first order of business, I would like to ask Curt something."

Surprised, Curt looked up at her and waited to hear what she had to say. Her hands were shaking. He'd already turned her down once, but she had to try one more time.

"Curt, I'd be honored if you'd be my date to the Homecoming Dance next Saturday night," Elle said. "What do you say?"

The audience collectively held its breath. Elle waited too, tensely. She was taking a chance. She was risking huge public humiliation, asking Curt to the dance in front of the entire school.

Curt moved his mouth, but Elle couldn't hear what he said.

"What did you say?" she asked.

"I said yes," Curt shouted. "Yes. I've lost the election. I'm not president anymore. But I'm looking forward to going to my first dance."

"Hooray!" The crowd roared. Elle waved at Curt and Merlin to join her on the stage and put an arm around each of them. They soaked in the applause. It had been a tough election, but in the end it had turned out well for everyone.

Chapter 23

"I'VE NEVER been out with a president before," Hunter said. He had taken Elle out to dinner to celebrate her victory. "I'm very proud of you," he added, and that made her happy . . . but a little nervous about the news she had to tell him.

"Thank you," Elle said. "You were a big help."

"I didn't do anything," Hunter said. "It was all you. This means the Homecoming Dance is on, right? What are you going to do? Do you have a date?"

"Well . . . kind of," she said.

"Uh-oh. Who is it? Let me guess—that kid who won Homecoming King?"

"No, he's going with Chessie," Elle said. "I want

you to understand, I did this for purely political reasons. It's not a real date. It's completely platonic. Just friends. I could never go out with this guy— he's too serious, not very good at having fun."

"Who is this Romeo?" Hunter asked.

"Curt Blaylock. My rival. I felt sorry for him losing, and I wanted to show him how wrong he was to try to cancel all the dances. And I know the only reason he did that was because he never had a date . . . so I volunteered myself." She watched Hunter's face. Was he mad? Upset?

"Curt Blaylock? The enemy?" Hunter said. "You're going with him?"

"Um, yes?" Elle was afraid to say it too definitely.

"And you think I'm going to be jealous of him?"

"Well . . . I don't know," Elle said.

Hunter laughed. "Don't worry, it's fine. It's very nice of you, Elle. That's my sweet girl."

Elle could breathe again. "Good, I'm so relieved! There's no reason for you to be jealous, but I didn't want you to worry—"

"I'm not worried about Curt," he said. "Besides, I understand. You're the president now. You've got responsibilities. You've got to make sacrifices for the good of the school."

"That's what I was thinking," Elle said.

He took her hand. "I am a little worried about one thing," he said. "My sweetie is at school without me this year. Someone *could* take you away from me. Not Curt, but someone."

"That won't happen," Elle said. "I'm too crazy about you."

"Even when you hardly ever get to see me?"

"I still think about you all the time."

"I think about you all the time, too."

"Some college girl could snag you away from me, too, you know," Elle said.

"But she won't," Hunter said. "Go to the dance, and have fun with Curt, if you can. I only hope he won't ruin it for you. Homecoming's one of the best nights of the year. Not as good as Prom, though."

"I wish you could be there with me."

"Me, too."

They kissed. Elle vowed to find a way to see Hunter more often, no matter how busy she got.

"I knew you could do it!" Bibi cried. "Congratulations!"

On Saturday morning Elle and Underdog had stepped into the Pamperella Salon for a predance makeover. Bibi had decorated her station with red, white, and blue bunting and a banner saying, HAIL TO THE CHIEF. She'd also taped a sign to her mirror that said, PRESIDENTIAL MANICURIST.

"Thank you," Elle said. "And thanks for all your help. This is for you." She presented Bibi with a box of Bernard's famous sugar cookies.

"Delicious!" Bibi declared, taking one. "Sit down, sit down. You've got a big night ahead of you. What's Hunter wearing?"

"Hunter can't go," Elle said. "I'm going with Curt."

Bibi made a face. "Your rival? The guy who wanted to get rid of the dances? Why?"

"He didn't have a date," Elle said. "And neither did I."

"Well, I think you could have done better," Bibi said. "This presents a tricky cosmetological problem." She studied Elle in the mirror. "You're going to a dance—that means glitter and glamour—but you're going as the new school president. Which says sober and sensible. Also, you're going with a guy you're not romantically interested in. . . . You're not, are you?"

Elle shook her head. "Definitely not."

"Thank goodness," Bibi said. "So you don't want to be too alluring, or he'll fall in love with you. On the other hand—back to square one—you're going to a dance. And who doesn't want to sparkle at a dance?"

"It's a tough one," Elle admitted.

"We can handle it," Bibi said. "What's your dress look like?"

Elle showed her a Polaroid of the dress she'd picked out—black lace, a full tea-length skirt, three-quarter sleeves, off the shoulder. "I'm wearing it with black satin pumps and long black gloves," she said.

"I love it," Bibi said. "Very Grace Kelly. Glamorous, yet serious. Just like the new prez. Black is great for a classic blonde like you. I wouldn't have suggested it before, because you were too young for it. But now . . . well, you've earned it, Elle. You're ready to wear black."

Elle flushed with pride. She'd taken a step forward in fashion maturity—a big step forward.

"Let's see what we can do with this," Bibi said. "Deep red nails, deep red lips, very matte makeup, and smooth, shiny hair. Agreed?"

"You're the expert," Elle said, but it sounded perfect to her.

Chapter 24

"ELLE, SOME boy is here," Eva said on the night of the Homecoming Dance. "He says he's your date."

"Right," Elle said. "That's Curt."

"Are you aware that he's dressed in a powder-blue tuxedo?" Eva said.

"He is?" That was unfortunate, Elle thought.

"Honey, tell me again why Hunter couldn't take you."

"It's okay, Mom," Elle said. "Going to Homecoming with a guy in a powder-blue tux won't kill me."

"Elle, he's wearing brown shoes," Eva said. "*Light* brown."

"Mom, I'll be fine."

"I just hate to see you backslide, after all the progress you've made," Eva said. "Stylewise, I mean."

"It's just this once," Elle said. "After tonight you'll never have to look at a pair of light brown shoes again."

"I hope not," Eva said. "By the way, this came for you today. Zosia forgot to tell me."

She gave Elle a box wrapped in blue-flowered paper. It was from the Rodeo Drive florist.

Elle read the card. *Have a good time tonight— but not too good a time,"* it said. *"Wish I could be there with you. I'll be thinking of you while I toil away in the lab. Love, Hunter."*

She felt warm all over. Hunter was so sweet! She unwrapped the box. Inside was a beautiful white corsage. "Mom, look." She showed the box and the note to her mother.

"What a love," Eva said. "Now *there's* a boy for you. Let me help you put it on."

Eva pinned the corsage to Elle's black lace dress. "It goes perfectly. How did he know?"

Elle shrugged. "He's just brilliant, I guess." But she wondered if Hunter had gotten a call from Bibi. It was just a hunch.

Eva stepped back to give her daughter a

once-over. "You look charming, honey. Have a good time tonight. And tell that boy out there that I won't let him back in this house until he's had a major fashion overhaul."

"Got it." She kissed her mother and floated into the living room to greet Curt. He swallowed hard when he saw her.

"Wow, you look more beautiful than Princess Leia in the first *Star Wars*," he said.

"Thank you."

He glanced at her corsage. "Oh, good, you've already got one of those. I forget to pick one up."

"No problem. Ready to go?"

"Ready."

The gym had been transformed into a blue-and-gold dream. A painted canvas was stretched over the ceiling to make it look like a starry, moonlit-night sky. The tables and chairs had been spray-painted gold, and a blue-and-gold banner said, HOMECOMING VICTORY. The football team had won the big game that day, so everyone was in a good mood.

"Isn't it wonderful?" Elle said.

"The social committee's budget on this was insane," Curt said, shaking his head. "I mean, it looks nice and all, but just think of all the other things we could have done with that money."

"What? What could we have done with it?" Elle asked.

"Improve the computer facilities, perhaps," Curt said. "Buy more books for the library. The science fiction section is woefully lacking in early Asimov."

"You still haven't learned your lesson, have you?" Elle said. "Even after losing the election."

"Hey—I concede the election to you. You won fair and square. As far as I could tell. But that wasn't a typical election. It got crazy, with all the love affairs and matchmaking—"

"I won because the kids disagreed with you," Elle said. "They like dances. Now, come on in, and try to have a good time. I bet by the end of the evening you will be converted. You will love dances."

"I'll take that bet," Curt said. "What are the stakes?"

Elle cast her eyes about the room for something to bet. She saw the photo booth, where couples could commemorate the evening with a picture.

"If I win, you have to have your picture taken in your tuxedo. We'll post it all over the school for a week," Elle said. "As president, I will insist on using your picture as the official announcement poster for the next dance—the winter dance."

"What?"

"Your Homecoming picture will be on a poster saying, 'Curt Blaylock says: Everybody come to the winter dance.' Or something like that. And I get to stand behind you while you're having your picture taken and give you rabbit ears. Okay?"

"No rabbit ears," Curt said.

"Okay," Elle said. "Fair enough."

"What if I win?" Curt said. "What if I have a terrible time tonight?"

"If you win . . ." Elle couldn't think of a prize he might like.

"If I win, I get to kiss you at the end of the night," Curt said.

"Curt, I don't know . . ." Elle said. "I told you, I have a boyfriend—"

"Just one kiss," Curt said. "Come on, if you're so sure I'm going to love this dance, then what's the risk?"

"But you could have a good time and then pretend you didn't, just to get the kiss," Elle said.

"I could, but I won't," Curt said. "I swear to you as an honorable person and a former school president. We're colleagues now, you and I. Political leaders of Beverly Hills High."

Elle liked that idea. "Okay, I'll take your word for it," Elle said. "As a fellow president."

"Hey, you guys." Laurette walked up, leading her boyfriend, Darren, by the hand. Like Hunter, Darren was in college, but he'd come back to take his girl to the dance.

Elle knew he must like Laurette a lot, because Darren was a rocker and thought he was too cool for dances. But maybe the previous year's Prom had changed his mind.

Darren bowed before Elle. "Mademoiselle President," he said, kissing her hand. "I'm sorry I graduated too soon to be at school during your administration."

"You're going to miss a wild year," Elle said.

"Hey, Curt, stylin' vintage seventies threads!" Laurette said. "You look like Mitchell Beckenheimer without the curly poodle perm."

"Who's Mitchell Beckenheimer?" Curt asked.

"My mom's Prom date from 1976."

"Oh. Thanks," Curt said. He looked at Elle to see whether he was supposed to be insulted or pleased.

"Coming from Laurette, it's a compliment," Elle told him.

"Coming from Chessie . . . that might be another story," Laurette said.

"Speaking of Chessie—is she here yet?" Elle wanted to see if she was having a good time with her dream date, Chris Rodriguez.

"Of course," Laurette said. "Homecoming Dude can't be late to the dance, and neither can his consort."

People filed into the gym to the beat of a DJ's music. Chessie plucked Chris's golden crown off his head and put it on her own head. It was a little too big for her. Then she dragged him onto the dance floor. Chris was happy to let Chessie wear his crown, since, he said, he felt like a dweeb in it.

"Look at her go," Laurette said.

Chessie bumped and lurched and stepped all over Chris's feet.

"Come on, let's go dance, too." Elle took Curt by the hand and pulled him onto the dance floor. Laurette and Darren followed.

Curt moved stiffly at first but loosened up as the dance floor got crowded and he got the hang of it.

"Are you having fun yet?" Elle asked.

Curt's grin disappeared. "No," he said. *Liar,* Elle thought.

"You look nice," Chessie told Elle. "A little extra makeup really helps hide your flaws."

"Thanks," Elle said.

The dance floor was packed. Elle spotted Merlin and Maggie boogying in a corner. Now that the campaign was over they could be open about their love at last.

Soon Curt and Elle were surrounded by Curt's friends: Craig Jenkins (with P.J.), Mike Mott (with Lisi), and Alan (with Tiina).

"This isn't so bad, is it, Curt?" Alan said. "I mean, when you've got a cute girl with you."

Tiina grinned, even though she had no idea what Alan was saying.

"It's okay," Curt said. Elle began to worry. Would he refuse to admit he was having a good time? Would she lose the bet? This was one evening she did not want to have end with a kiss.

The music stopped, and Mr. Wrightsman took the microphone.

"Everyone, be seated. We have a few ceremonial rituals to take care of, and then you can get back to the fun."

"Let's all get a big table together," Elle said to Curt. They herded all his friends and their dates and Laurette and Darren to a big round table at the side of the room.

"First of all, I'd like to say congratulations to Chris and Chloe, our freshly crowned King and

Queen. Let's give them a big hand."

Everyone clapped and cheered as Chloe and Chris mounted the stage and waved to their subjects. Chloe tried to grab Chris's hand, but he pulled it away.

"Poor Chessie," Laurette whispered. "She's going to have to spend the whole night defending her turf."

"They'll be having their official Homecoming Dance in just a few moments," Mr. Wrightsman said. "But first, I'd also like to congratulate our brand-new student body president, Elle Woods! Elle, come on up here."

Elle took the stage as everyone cheered her on. She waved and said, "It's an honor. I'm so excited!" And she was. Now that she stood on the stage in her official capacity as president and looked at all the people depending on her to lead them, she shivered. She was nervous but happy. She knew she could do it if she put her whole heart into it.

As she walked off the stage, everyone in the room stood up and clapped for her in a standing ovation. She was touched and overwhelmed. Kids reached out to shake her hand as she passed through the crowd and returned to her table.

"Wow, Elle," Laurette said. "You're already the

most popular president the school has ever seen—at least since we've been here."

"This job is a sacred trust," Elle said. "Right, Curt?"

"Sure," Curt said. "But you also get to boss people around a lot, if that's what you're into."

"That was always Curt's favorite perk," Alan joked.

"You'll have to choose a cabinet," Curt told Elle. "Advisers, people you trust. You need a treasurer and a secretary, but you can add other posts as necessary. Craig there was my cafeteria czar. His job was to work on improving the food."

"What happened?" P.J. said. "The food hasn't changed at all. You really slacked off, didn't you, Craig?"

"The cafeteria is a bureaucratic nightmare," Craig said. "*You* try getting the cook to learn nouvelle cuisine."

"Ladies and gentlemen, by popular decree, the Homecoming Queen and the Homecoming King!" Mr. Wrightsman announced.

Chloe and Chris, crowns on their head (Chris had to struggle to rip his out of Chessie's hands), danced their official dance to a slow song. Everyone else sat at their tables and watched. When the song was half over, Mr. Wrightsman said, "Everybody, get up and join them on the dance floor!"

"Please," Chris said. "Somebody, join us."

Chessie wormed her way between Chris and Chloe and pressed herself against Chris.

Suzanne Marconi, a tall, shy girl in a plain blue dress, walked up to Elle's table. Suzanne had been the treasurer in Curt's cabinet. She stood in front of Curt, her brown hair hiding her face as usual. She brushed the hair to the side and tucked it behind her ear. *She's pretty*, Elle thought.

Suzanne looked Curt in the eye. "Will you dance with me?"

Curt blinked at her, surprised. Then he looked at Elle. "Would you mind?"

"Of course not," Elle said. "Go. Dance."

He stood up and followed Suzanne to the dance floor.

"I always thought she kind of liked him," Mike said. "But she's so shy—I never thought she'd get up the nerve to do something like that."

Elle watched them on the dance floor. Suzanne had seemed shy when she spoke but not when she danced. She threw her arms up in the air, wagged her hips, and bobbed her head like a *Soul Train* pro.

"She must take classes or something," Laurette said.

Curt and Suzanne danced together for the rest of the night, to Elle's relief. By the end of the evening, Curt looked like a different person. His normally neat hair was messy from dancing, his face was flushed, and he was grinning from ear to ear.

Now that she was free, lots of other boys asked Elle to dance. She danced with Laurette and Chessie and other friends, too. The cheerleaders made a victory circle around her, clapping and cheering to celebrate her presidency.

It wasn't the perfect romantic evening, the way the Senior Prom with Hunter had been, but that was okay. She wasn't looking for romance. Her fellow students had come together and voted to save one of their most important school traditions, and that made Elle happy. It showed that school spirit was alive and well at Beverly Hills High.

Finally the DJ said, "This is the last dance of the night, so choose your partner carefully."

Curt asked Elle to dance. "I thought I should acknowledge the girl who made all of this possible by having the last dance with you," Curt said.

"All of what possible?" Elle asked.

"Well . . ." His eyes trailed across the room to Suzanne, who was dancing with some girlfriends. Something had clicked, it seemed, and they'd fallen for each other.

"Are you having a good time?" Elle asked him. "You'd better tell the truth."

He hesitated. She knew it was hard for him to admit defeat, even on a silly bet. But a promise was a promise.

"I'm having the greatest time ever!" he said. "You were right—dances are good. I should have started coming to them in ninth grade. If I had, maybe I would have liked school a lot more."

"So I don't get a kiss at the end of the night?" Elle asked.

"Sorry, no kiss," Curt said. "I don't want to blow it with Suzanne."

"Will you do me a favor, then?" Elle said. "Will you help me learn how to be a good president?"

"If you'll make me your secretary of social life," Curt said. "I want to plan more dances. Lots and lots of dances!"

"It's a deal. Truce?"

"More than a truce." Curt took Elle's hand and shook it. "Friends."

"Friends," Elle said. She grabbed Laurette and Darren and Chessie and Chris; Curt grabbed Suzanne, and they ended the last dance in a big, happy circle of friends.

Here's a sneak peek at

Blonde Love

Chapter 1

Roses are red, magenta, maroon;
Valentine's Day is coming soon. Give
your love a lacy heart, and chocolates
if you're really smart; a fancy dinner
à la carte. Go, Bees!

"I DON'T see what that cheer has to do with basketball," Chessie Morton said, dropping her pom-pom on the floor.

"It doesn't," P. J. Stoller said.

"Yes, it does," Elle Woods said. "Love is part of everything. Even basketball."

"Oh, no," Chessie said. "Elle's been taken over by the Blonde Buddha again."

"It's not Buddhism," Elle said. "It's valentine fever! Let's try it one more time."

Elle led the cheerleading squad through the cheer once more. Most of the girls had the moves down already, but Chessie missed a step and kicked Chloe Gaitskill by mistake. Chloe gave her a dirty look.

"Okay, I guess we can quit for today," Elle said. "But let's practice extra hard tomorrow. We've got to get the new cheers down before the game on Friday."

Elle Woods, as the captain of the Beverly Hills High School cheerleading squad, was responsible for writing most of the cheers. Whatever was on her mind tended to come out in the rhymes. And love was on her mind.

Valentine's Day was only a few weeks away. And she had special plans.

The cheerleaders broke formation and went to the locker room. "Chloe, I love your new haircut," Chessie said.

Chloe's long straight blonde hair had once hung halfway down her back. Now it was chopped into chic shoulder-length blond chunks.

"Is that a Val?" Chessie asked.

"What's a Val?" Elle asked.

"You don't know what a Val is?" Chessie said. "Sometimes you're so out of it it's cute, Elle. You know, the Val. It's the hot new haircut, invented by Valerie Vernay, stylist to the stars?"

"Oh, right," Elle said. It all sounded vaguely familiar to her. "I think I saw that on *Access Hollywood*."

"My mother got me an appointment with Valerie Vernay herself," Chloe said. "Which is practically impossible. But Mom is friends with the head of Bluestone Pictures, so, you know . . ." Everybody knew. Her mom had pulled some strings. "I saw Tippi Hanover at the salon."

"You look just like Tippi now," Chessie said. "Only prettier."

Tippi Hanover was a rising teen star actress. Everyone wanted to look like her. She was one of the stars who had made Valerie Vernay famous.

"Thanks," said Chloe, happily taking the compliment. "I think I'll go to Pacifico tonight and show it off." Pacifico was a trendy dance club, very popular with Beverly Hills students.

"You're going to Pacifico?" Chessie said. "What a coincidence! I was going to go to Pacifico tonight, too. Let's go together."

Chloe shrugged. "Sure, whatever. Do you want

to come along, too, Elle?"

"I'd love to, but I'm busy," Elle said.

"Oh?" Chessie said. "Seeing Hunter tonight?"

Hunter Perry was Elle's boyfriend. He was a freshman at UCLA.

"I wish," Elle said. "He's got basketball practice, and then some kind of frat meeting. I've got to get ready for the student senate meeting tomorrow." In addition to being the captain of the cheerleaders, Elle was also student body president.

"You and Hunter are both so busy, I don't know how you ever see each other," Chloe said.

"It's hard," Elle said. "But we made a promise to see each other at least once a week, no matter what."

"You're smart to schedule your dates," Chessie said. "That way Hunter can't get out of them."

"I don't think he wants to get out of them," Elle said. "He told me he wishes he could see me more often."

"He was always such a flatterer," Chessie said. "Silver Tongue. That's what Savannah used to call him."

Savannah Shaw was the former cheerleading captain of Beverly Hills High—and Hunter's ex-girlfriend. She was the kind of girl every other girl wished she could be. But she'd graduated the year before. Even though she was gone, Chessie still liked to bring up her name once in a while. Elle didn't mind. It helped keep her on her toes.

Elle took off her cheer shorts and changed into designer jeans and a plaid blazer. "Wait till Hunter sees what I have planned for Valentine's Day."

She'd spent hours imagining that romantic evening. "We're going to have dinner at my house, out by the pool. Bernard will help me cook, and Zosia promised to help set up the table, with flowers and candles and everything, so it'll be superromantic."

Elle's parents lived in a beautiful modern house in Brentwood. It had a pool, of course, and servants' quarters. Bernard was their butler and Zosia their maid—but by now the two were more like family.

Elle imagined herself sitting with Hunter in the moonlight on a warm southern California evening, just the two of them, trading chocolate-covered strawberries and kisses. . . .

"That sounds so nice," P.J. said. "I wish Craig would do romantic things like that." She'd been going out with Craig Jenkins, but it wasn't serious. "I'll probably spend Valentine's Day at home watching *American Idol*."

"Matt's taking me to the Lakers game," Tamila Vines complained. Her boyfriend, Matt Reiss, was a basketball fanatic, but he was too short to make the Beverly Hills High team. So he had become manager instead. "He bought the tickets before he realized it was Valentine's Day."

"Everybody knows Valentine's Day is February fourteenth," P.J. said. "Spacing on that is so *boy*."

"Well, I'm going to do something fabulous on Valentine's Day," Chessie said.

"Really?" Elle said. "What?"

"I don't know yet," Chessie said. "But it's going to rock."

"Everybody should celebrate Valentine's Day, whether they're in love or not," Elle said. "I think there should be parties everywhere, all over the city, for everyone."

"Why don't we have a big party here at school?" Tamila said.

"That's a great idea," Elle said. "Maybe we will." As president, she had the power to get things like that done.

Chessie tightened the belt on her safari jacket. "Oh, Elle, I almost forgot to tell you. Guess who's friends with Hunter? My next-door neighbor, Julia Gables."

"Really?" Elle said. "That's a funny coincidence."

"I *know*," Chessie said. "She's a freshman at UCLA too, and they have *two* classes together, Sociology and Psych. Of course, as soon as I realized she was going to UCLA, I asked if she knew Hunter. Turns out they're good friends."

"Is she nice?" Elle asked.

"*So* nice," Chessie said. "And gorgeous. She's tall, with long dark hair and green eyes like a cat's. She kind of reminds me of Savannah, only not blonde."

Elle felt a twinge of jealousy, but it faded quickly. She had used to think that Savannah was Hunter's ideal girl. Hunter was tall, and so was Savannah. Elle was an adorable blonde with great taste in clothes, but she was on the petite side. But she and Hunter had been together for eight months now. She wasn't worried about tall girls anymore. She was over that now. Totally secure.

"I'm glad Hunter's making friends," Elle said. "Not that it's hard for him."

"Has he mentioned Julia to you?" Chessie asked.

"No," Elle said.

"That's funny," Chessie said. "Julia made it sound like she sees him all the time."

"He can't mention every person he meets at

school, Chessie," P.J. said.

"I know," Chessie said. "I'm just saying . . ."

"I'm not worried," Elle said. "I know Hunter loves me. And I trust him. One hundred percent."

"When's your next date?" Chessie asked.

"Saturday night," Elle said. "Three whole days away." It seemed like forever. Elle wished she could see Hunter every day.

"A lot can happen in three whole days," Chessie said.

"Yeah," Chloe said. "In three days you could get laryngitis and stop talking, Chessie."

"Chessie could never stop talking," P.J. said. "Even if she had her tongue surgically removed."

"I heard about this girl in Malibu who did that to make her cheekbones more prominent," Tamila said.

"What? No way," Chloe said. "That wasn't her tongue. It was her back teeth."

"Can you talk without your back teeth?" P.J. said.

"Of course," Chloe said. "But you can't eat as much, so it helps keep you thin, which makes your cheekbones stick out even more."

"Chessie could talk without her tongue, her teeth, or her lips," P.J. said. "If you sewed her mouth shut, she'd figure out a way to talk through her nose."

"Hey," Chessie said, looking hurt, "I'm not some kind of talking freak."

Elle felt sorry for her. "Don't pick on Chessie," she said. "She's only trying to give me a Hunter news flash. To be nice."

"Sure, she is," Chloe said.